T.S

"You ... you don't you

Stephanie's question was an agonized whisper.

"'Know,' Mrs. Hammond?" Maxim raised a dark satanic eyebrow as he looked at her with a bland, cool smile on his lips. "I know many things. What particular subject did you have in mind?"

He hasn't changed, she thought. Maxim had always been noted for conducting his financial and business affairs with a skill that was thoroughly Machiavellian. Now, she realized, he had merely refined his technique over the years.

Well, he wasn't going to play games with her, Stephanie told herself, as a deep tide of anger flowed through her veins. Maybe her safe secure world was about to disintegrate, but to be forced to dance on the end of a string manipulated by this man would be a far worse fate!

MARY LYONS is happily married to an Essex farmer, has two children and lives in an old Victorian rectory. Life is peaceful—unlike her earlier years when she worked as a radio announcer, reviewed books and even ran for parliament in a London dockland area. She still loves a little excitement and combines romance with action and suspense in her books whenever possible.

Books by Mary Lyons

HARLEQUIN PRESENTS

Don't miss any of our special offers. Write to us at the following address for information on our newest releases.

Harlequin Reader Service
901 Fuhrmann Blvd., P.O. Box 1397, Buffalo, NY 14240
Canadian address: P.O. Box 603,
Fort Erie, Ont. L2A 5X3

MARY LYONS

love in a spin

Harlequin Books

TORONTO • NEW YORK • LONDON
AMSTERDAM • PARIS • SYDNEY • HAMBURG
STOCKHOLM • ATHENS • TOKYO • MILAN

Harlequin Presents first edition June 1990
ISBN 0-373-11276-9

Original hardcover edition published in 1989
by Mills & Boon Limited

CHAPTER ONE

'SAY—how about another drink?'

Stephanie shook her blonde head, smiling at the middle-aged man as she put a slim, delicate hand over her glass. 'Not for me, Harold. I've got to drive myself home in a minute.'

'Aw, come on, Stephanie. Just a small brandy to seal our deal, hmm?'

'Good heavens, no—one glass of wine on top of an empty stomach is *quite* enough!' she laughed. 'But I am, as always, very grateful for the large order you've just given me. And not having to fly to the States on a selling trip is a great bonus. In fact, maybe I should buy you a drink, instead?'

'Heaven forbid!' Harold Finberg got to his feet. 'The day I let a woman pick up the tab is the day when I *know* I'm ready for the old folks' home!' he said with a twinkle in his eye, before going over to the bar.

He really liked staying in this hotel, deep in the English countryside. With its oak-panelled walls and large, open fireplaces filled with glowing logs, it always struck him as a genuine piece of old England. It was expensive, of course. But what the heck—if you wanted the best these days, you had to pay for it.

Just like the knitwear designed and produced

by Stephanie, he mused thoughtfully, glancing back at the girl sitting beside one of the old, mullioned windows. It never ceased to amaze him that the daughter of one of his old classmates—whom—he'd first seen in her pram, for heaven's sake!—should have matured into such a talented and beautiful woman.

The discreet lighting in the bar couldn't dim the gleam of her long, thick ash-blonde hair, loosely piled up in a heavy knot on top of her head; or the wide, misty blue eyes which dominated her slim face, whose pale, creamy skin glowed with health. Oh, yes—the little Stephanie he'd once known had now become a truly beautiful woman, all right. So how come she'd never got married again?

The question was still on his mind as he walked back to the table.

'I've been thinking—how long is it since you've been living in the Cotswolds?' he asked. 'I know it's four or five years since we bumped into each other, here in the high street.'

'Yes—I can still remember the shock!' she grinned. 'I couldn't believe it was really you—not when we'd last seen each other well over three thousand miles away in New York. Still, I guess it was my lucky day,' she added, raising her glass to him. 'Because, although I've had the shop for the past seven years, it wasn't till I met you again that my business really took off in America.'

'Your distribution is worldwide now, honey,'

he corrected with satisfaction. 'And I reckon your latest designs will do us both a power of good.'

Stephanie beamed at her father's old friend. Harold was first and foremost a businessman. As a supplier to department stores all over the world, she knew—old friend or not—that if she hadn't been able to supply the high-class, handmade knitwear demanded by his customers, then it would have been a case of: 'Sorry—no sale.'

'So, OK—you've had your shop and knitwear business in the village of Broadway for the last seven years. Haven't you ever thought of getting married again?'

'Whatever for?' Stephanie looked at him in surprise. 'I've got such a full life. There's my business, of course, and also the three children to look after—although Richard and Claire are grown up now, of course,' she corrected herself. 'But Adam's only nine, and although he's away at school during the week, I can tell you that after a weekend spent with the little genius I'm mentally worn out!' she laughed. 'So how could I possibly cope with a husband as well?'

'But that's the whole point,' he persisted. 'If you found a nice guy, he could take some of the load off your shoulders. You were married for what . . .?'

'Almost three years.'

'So those older kids are your stepchildren, right?'

'Yes, but I love them—every bit as much as if they were my own children,' she protested.

'Sure you do,' Harold said, leaning forward to pat her hand. 'But it must have been heavy-going to look after two teenagers when your husband died; not to mention leaving London to start a shop up here, *and* fixing up that crazy old barn you live in.' He patted her hand again. 'I know losing your parents when you were so young can't have been easy—heaven knows, that air crash was really tragic—but won't you accept some fatherly advice from me, and give yourself a break, Stephanie? After all, you're only what . . . twenty-seven?'

'Twenty-nine,' she admitted ruefully.

Harold shrugged. 'So, who's counting? You look damn good to me. And you ought to find yourself a man—if only for Adam's sake. He may be as bright as can be, but I guess he's like every other little boy that I've ever known. He needs a father.'

A brief, painful shadow dimmed her misty blue eyes for a moment. 'Yes, I . . . I know that what you're saying makes sense, but . . . OK, OK—I'll think about it!' she said hastily when it looked as if he was going to keep pressing the point. 'Now, how's your business doing?' she asked, determined to change the subject. She had made one marriage of convenience, and although James Hammond had been a sweet, kind man she knew that she could never enter into such an arrangement ever again.

She loved Richard and Claire, of course, and her stepchildren's pleasure and delight in Adam's birth nine years ago had helped to cement and bond together the original, slightly shaky foundations of her marriage. Over the years their relationships with one another had been forged into a secure, family unit which even the devastation of James's tragically early death had failed to dent. To marry again—even if it meant giving her son a father—wasn't the simple answer to any problems she might have. For one thing, Adam would undoubtedly resent and be irritated by anyone less clever than himself, and as far as she was concerned—well, her heart had been broken beyond repair a long, long time ago.

'. . . So, all in all, it's been one hell of a year!'

'Hmm?' Stephanie muttered, realising that while she'd been buried deep in thought she had missed much of what Harold was saying. 'I'm sorry—I was daydreaming,' she confessed with a guilty smile. 'What was the problem?'

'Well, as I said, I'd always thought my business was as safe as houses, but I made the crass error of giving some shares to my wife's brothers. You know how it is,' he grinned sheepishly. 'She kept yakking on about "blood being thicker than water", and how we should keep the business in the family——' He shrugged.

'So, what happened?'

Harold sighed. 'It was the worst decision of my life. Those two good-for-nothing cheapskates didn't wait five minutes before dumping the shares on the market, and before I knew what was happening, I had the Grant-Tyler Corporation trying to gobble up my business.'

'What . . .?'

'Yeah, you may well look shocked. I nearly gave up the ghost there and then! We all know about Maxim Tyler—right? Well, maybe over here in England you don't get all the news on Wall Street,' he added as she stared at him with dazed, blank eyes. 'But you can take it from me, that when that ruthless bastard decides he wants a company—that's it! Well, as you can imagine, I put up a bit of a fight, but even I knew the writing was on the wall. And then—glory be— Maxim suddenly backed off,' Harold gave her a wide grin. 'It seems Grant-Tyler had another big deal on the go, and I subsequently heard that they'd grabbed hold of some large British finance company instead. But I tell you, kid, it was a close shave!'

'Yes . . .er . . .yes, I can see it must have been,' she said in a flat, toneless voice.

'Still, now I'm off the hook, I don't mind admitting that you've got to hand it to the guy,' Harold said, leaning back in his chair and lighting a large cigar. 'It may have been his wife's money to start with—they say that Estelle Grant was *loaded*—but there's no doubt that Maxim would have made it on his own, without any backing. Yeah, that guy's a real killer—

businesswise,' he added, blowing a smoke ring up at the ceiling.

Stephanie jumped quickly to her feet. 'I . . .I have to go. I must get home, and . . .'

'Hey—are you all right, honey?' Harold asked, looking anxiously at her chalk-white face. 'I'm sorry, it's all my fault. I shouldn't have lit that damn cigar.'

'No . . . no, it's not that. It's just . . . well, it really is late, and . . . and I've got some designs I want to check over before . . . before giving them to the outworkers,' she gabbled breathlessly, quickly pulling on her woollen cape. 'It's been lovely seeing you,' she added, giving him a quick peck on the cheek. 'I'll be in touch—OK? Bye.'

And, leaving Harold gazing after her with stunned surprise, Stephanie bolted from the room.

Standing on the pavement outside the Lygon Arms, Stephanie shivered with cold, and wished that she'd put on something warmer for her meeting with Harold than the elegant, sapphire-blue, thinly woven cashmere dress. Its matching cape was undoubtedly very dashing, but it offered little defence against the cold, blustery March wind.

Crossing the road, she walked quickly past the village green, and into the shelter of the shopping arcade which led to the car park. Normally the sight of her own shop, *The Spinning Wheel*, with its elegant display of sweaters in toning shades of soft mauve and lilac, would have given her a considerable sense of pleasure. But not tonight. She hardly bothered to glance at the goods so artistically arranged in the softly lit bow window. Like an animal in pain, her first and only instinct was to reach warmth and shelter—to crawl into a dark burrow until the agony eased, and she could begin trying to face life again.

It was bound to happen sooner or later, Stephanie told herself as her cold, shivering fingers fumbled with the car keys. Even all those years ago, Maxim Tyler's strong, dominant personality had swept all before him, so she might have guessed that such a forceful, dynamic character wasn't likely to remain in the shadows. And now that he was, according to what Harold had said, becoming a considerable force in the financial business world . . . well, she was obviously going to have to get used to hearing about him, and seeing his name in the newspapers.

But that was easier said than done, she thought, finally managing to unlock the car door, feeling sick and shivering like a leaf as she eased herself into the driving seat.

Eventually she managed to regain some measure of self-control. And the belated realisation that Harold had been talking about the American stock market also helped to calm her worst fears. After all, she told herself firmly as she drove carefully out of the car park, there was a whole world of difference between Wall Street and the City of London—not to mention the broad expanse of the Atlantic Ocean in between. And even if Maxim had caused her so much pain and heartbreak in the past—that had been a good ten years ago. Leaving her own fears aside, he had undoubtedly forgotten all about their brief affair. So it was quite plainly ridiculous for her to become panic-stricken with alarm and dismay at the mere mention of his name.

Continuing to sternly lecture herself over the next five miles, she had more or less recovered her usual equilibrium by the time she turned into the gateway which led to the Old Barn, only to be thrown into panic as she saw the dim glow of lights shining behind the drawn curtains of her empty house.

A moment later the front door was thrown open, lamplight spilling out on to the flagstones and illuminating a tall, slim figure standing in the doorway.

'Ah, here you are at last! Where on earth have you been?'

'Hi, darling.' Stephanie almost sagged with relief, giving her stepdaughter a quick hug before walking through into the hall. 'Heavens, Claire—you gave me a fright! I didn't see your car—I guess you must have put it away in the garage—so when I drove up just now and saw all these lights on in the house, I nearly had hysterics. I was sure it was burglars, or . . .'

'A burglary—in this village? In Stow-under-Hill? You must be joking!' Claire gave a short bark of wry laughter as she helped Stephanie off with her cape. 'Even now she's dead, I bet old Mrs Wensley-Pritchard's ghost still patrols the village—and that would be quite enough to frighten off even the most determined robber.'

Stephanie grinned. 'I know she was a real pain in the neck, but now she's gone, I kind of miss the old dragon. I wonder what's going to happen to the manor house and the estate?'

'That's just what I . . .'

'Oh, thank you, darling,' Stephanie exclaimed, walking through into the large sitting-room and finding that her stepdaughter had lit a roaring log fire. 'Hmm . . . this is just wonderful!' she purred, sinking down on to a pile of cushions beside the large inglenook fireplace.

'It was such a freezing cold day that I thought I'd better try and heat the place up before you came home,' Claire said, and moved over towards a table in the corner of the large room. 'How about a brandy to warm you up?'

'Well . . .' Stephanie hesitated. 'OK—why not? Just a small one,' she murmured, bending forward to warm her cold hands at the fire. 'And now—pleased as I am to see you—what on earth are you doing up here in the middle of the week? I do hope . . . is everything all right with your job?' she asked tentatively.

She loved the girl, but there was no doubt that

Claire could be prickly and difficult at times, a victim of strong emotions over which she did not always have one hundred per cent control. However, since going to university to study economics, her stepdaughter's volatile temperament had matured into a far more content, calmer disposition. And now that Claire was living in London, and working for an international finance corporation in the City, Stephanie had been hopeful that all the girl's worries and uncertainties were now well behind her.

Claire shook her head. 'There's no problem at work—quite the reverse. For the last few months I've been acting as a personal assistant to the Great White Chief himself, *and* I've had a whacking rise in salary!' she grinned. 'In fact, workwise, it's all systems go.'

'Hey—that's great news!' Stephanie beamed at her. 'However, pardon me if I'm wrong, but do I detect a new, transatlantic influence—"workwise"—in my dear daughter's conversation?' she queried blandly. 'It sure will be a nice change not to have *my* English constantly corrected by a toffee-nosed, plummy-voiced female who . . .'

She didn't get any further, both of them laughing as she caught the cushion thrown at her by the younger girl.

'Seriously though, Stephanie, the reason I'm here is . . .'

'Hang on a moment. If you want to have a

serious talk, then I'm all ears,' she assured
Claire. 'However, it's been a long day, and I'm
absolutely starving. So how about if I fix us up
something nice and hot to eat, and then you can
tell all?'

'That sounds fine. Do you want some help?'

'No, you sit by the fire, and I'll give you a
shout when I'm ready,' Stephanie said, getting
to her feet and making her way through into the
kitchen.

Thank heavens for the Aga! she thought,
relishing the warmth of the red enamelled stove
as she moved a beef casserole in the top oven.
When they'd first moved up here from London,
there had been very little money left from the
purchase of both the shop and their new
home—and putting in such an expensive stove
had been madly extravagant. But her
grandmother's old kitchen range back home in
America had always been the centre of family life
for as long as she could remember, and she had
never regretted the purchase of an item which
had the added merit of always keeping the
kitchen as warm as toast.

So much had happened during the last seven
years, it was hard to remember just what a mess
this place had once been. Although that was
why she had managed to buy it so cheaply, of
course. No one with any sense would have taken
on the amount of work required to turn the
large, decrepit old cattle barn into a home. But
she had been fascinated to learn that the honey-

gold Cotswold stone building had been constructed from the remains of an old priory, which had originally stood on the site. The Dissolution of the Monasteries in the sixteenth century had put paid to the priory, of course, and when the main highway between Cheltenham and Evesham had been re-routed, one hundred years later, a once thriving community had been left cut off, and slumbering peacefully for the next three centuries.

And what was going to happen to Stow-under-Hill, now that old Mrs Wensley-Pritchard had finally—at the ripe old age of ninety-two—gone to join her ancestors? It didn't matter a hoot to her, of course, Stephanie told herself thankfully, since she owned the freehold of the Old Barn. But for the rest of the village it was a very different story. Not only had Mrs Wensley-Pritchard held the Lordship of the Manor of Stow, but she had also owned the whole of the village—*lock, stock and barrel*!

It seemed an extraordinary anachronism, in this day and age, that anyone should actually own a whole community. And it wasn't just all the houses, of course. The estate, amounting to about five thousand acres of prime farm land, also included the local inn, the Cross Keys, the village post office and general store, a small primary school and even the Reverend David Lower's old Georgian rectory.

'Is supper ready yet?' Claire asked, coming into the kitchen. 'You're not the only one who's starving—I'm hungry enough to eat a horse!'

'Yes, sorry, I was daydreaming,' Stephanie said, taking the casserole out of the oven and placing it on the scrubbed pine table in the middle of the large room. 'Actually, I was just wondering what's going to happen to the village. I'd have thought that everyone here would have jumped at the thought of buying their own home, but not a bit of it!'

'Well, I was trying to . . .'

'Wouldn't you want to be able to choose the colour of your own front door?' Stephanie continued, barely noticing the other girl's interjection. 'Sure you would. And yet that old dragon used to give everyone hell if they so much as planted different flowers in their front garden!'

'Oh, come on—I know she was a dreadful old tyrant, but that's a huge exaggeration!'

'Not much of one, it isn't,' Stephanie retorted grimly. 'Don't you remember all that fuss—about the painted sign hanging up outside the pub? In the end, poor Tom Watson had to do as old Mrs Wensley-Pritchard said, and take it down, she added indignantly. 'And yet, according to Tilly, everyone in the village is hoping and praying that the National Trust or some other large organisation will buy up the whole estate.'

'Well, if it keeps the village unspoiled, then I suppose their feelings are fairly understandable. In fact, if you really think about it, it's far and away the best solution.'

Stephanie shook her head. 'If it was just to keep out the property speculators, I'd agree that it might be a good idea. But it isn't just that. The villagers apparently *want* things to go on the way they always have, ever since the year dot. I know some people might think that it's a cute idea. But quite honestly, Claire, if I live in England until I'm a hundred and two, I still won't be able to understand why it is that you British go for all that sort of crazy feudal nonsense!'

The younger girl looked at her with startled eyes. 'I didn't realise . . . I mean, you really do feel strongly about it, don't you?'

'Sure I do. I'm American, aren't I?' demanded Stephanie aggressively. 'What do you think our War of Independence was all about? As I told Tilly—I reckon this village ought to have itself a Boston Tea Party!' she added darkly.

'Hey—calm down! It isn't like you to get so steamed up. Is there anything worrying you?' Claire asked with concern.

'No—no, of course not,' Stephanie said quickly. 'It's just . . . I guess it's been a long day and I'm tired, that's all.'

Claire grinned at her. 'If I remember my history correctly, I think the last peasants' revolt was in 1381. So, if things haven't changed in the last six hundred years, I don't suppose that you're going to be able to do much about it!'

Stephanie gave a wry laugh. 'You're quite

right, I'm not. So we'd better leave the revolting peasants to their fate, and get on with our supper.'

'Now you're talking! That's the best idea I've heard all day,' the younger girl agreed, fetching knives, forks and plates from the large, old Welsh dresser against the far wall of the kitchen. 'By the way, how is Tilly?' she asked. 'Are her feet still killing her?'

Stephanie smiled at the accurate mimicry of her old housekeeper's Worcestershire accent. 'Tilly loves to have a good grumble. In fact, she informed me only yesterday that her bunions were, as she put it, ''acting up something chronic''!'

'I don't know why you put up with her,' Claire muttered as they sat down at the table. 'She used to drive me up the wall in five minutes flat—although she always had a soft spot for Richard.'

'Ah, well, she was very good to us when we first came to the village . . .' Stephanie shrugged. 'Incidentally, did I tell you that I had a letter from Richard yesterday?'

'A letter?' Claire raised her eyebrows. 'Since my dear brother never sets pen to paper if he can possibly help it—he must want something! Is he all right?'

'Fine, from all accounts. He's enjoying the job with the oil company, and says the set-up in the Alaskan oil fields has to be seen to be believed. However,' Stephanie gave her a rueful smile, 'you're quite right. Your brother's letter was mostly concerned with an urgent request for some warm sweaters!'

'And you, being the good stepmother that you are, will undoubtedly send off a huge consignment!'

Stephanie's cheeks coloured slightly. 'Well, I did think that I might design something for him,' she admitted. 'A white polar bear on a black background might be rather fun, don't you think? Or maybe a map of Alaska, showing the pipeline running across the State?' she murmured, picking up a pencil and making a lightning sketch on the large drawing-pad which she always kept on the table.

Claire shook her head, smiling fondly at the girl who was only eight years older than herself. 'You always did spoil him rotten—and me, too, for that matter,' she added, helping herself to some more beef and potatoes from the earthenware casserole.

'I don't know about spoiling you both, but I do know that I've already had something knitted up for you.'

'Really? That's great! What's the design?'

'With your clarinet in mind, I thought musical notes would be appropriate, so the sweater is covered with crochets, minims and quavers! It's upstairs in your room. Why don't you try it on while I make the coffee?'

Stephanie smiled to herself as the younger girl jumped to her feet and hurried from the kitchen.

Music had always been an important part of Claire's life and, although her stepdaughter wasn't talented enough to have pursued a soloist's career, she still gained considerable pleasure in playing with an amateur orchestra in London. However, if there was one thing she'd learnt as a stepmother, it was the important principle of 'fair shares for all'. And even now, when the children were grown up and out in the big wide world, it seemed that the same basic law held true.

Underneath all her apparent cool sophistication, Claire was still the same little girl who had kept such a beady, jealous eye on her brother, making sure that he never got a larger slice of the cake than she did.

When she had first married James Hammond, both Richard and Claire—then aged thirteen and eleven—had been lonely, unhappy children who had rejected all of Stephanie's first, hesitant advances, determined to cling to the memory of their mother who had died so recently. However, with the passage of time, and the slow realisation that she had no intention of trying to take the place of their mother in their hearts, both children had relaxed their guard. Now, ten years later, it was difficult to remember a time when they hadn't been a tight, warm family circle.

Carrying the coffee tray into the sitting room, Stephanie sank down once more in her favourite place by the fireside, pulling her drawing-board

on to her lap. It was no good trying to hide the
fact from herself, she was still feeling disturbed
and upset by her conversation with Harold.
And, as always at such times, she knew that the
panacea for such problems was to bury herself in
work. In fact, so absorbed did she become that
she hardly noticed Claire's return.

'It's a lovely jumper, thank you so much.'

'That's all right, honey. Pour yourself some
coffee,' she murmured, concentrating on a
particularly intricate detail.

'. . . so I said that I'd show him around the
village. I truly had no idea that you felt so
strongly, or I wouldn't have suggested . . . Oh,
for goodness' sake—*Stephanie*!'

'Hmm?'

'I've been talking to you for the last five
minutes,' Claire exclaimed with annoyance.
'You haven't been listening to a *thing* I've been
saying!'

'What's the problem?' she muttered, not
taking her eyes off the pad in front of her.

Claire gave a heavy sigh. 'Honestly—you're
impossible! I ought to know by now that once
you've got a pen or pencil in your hands, you're
simply not *compos mentis*! But do please try and
concentrate—just for once?'

It was the constrained, oddly nervous note in
her stepdaughter's voice which broke through
Stephanie's absorption in the new design she
was creating. Raising her blond head, she stared
at the girl sitting across the room. 'Is this why

you've come up here today from London?'

'Yes. I've been trying to explain ever since I arrived, but I kept getting side-tracked. It's my boss, you see. I said that I'd show him around, and that we'd maybe call in and see you. I do realise *now* that you hate the whole idea of anyone ''owning'' the village, but I didn't know that at the time, did I? I just wanted to be helpful. It's really quite important and . . . well, it seemed such a good idea . . .' Her voice trailed miserably away.

Stephanie put down her drawing-pad. 'I'm sorry, honey, but I'm getting a mite confused. If you want to show your boss around the village—what's the problem? And if you both want to call in here, that's fine too. I'll be pleased to see him.'

'But that's the whole point—I don't think you will.' Claire took a deep breath. 'The fact is, old Mrs Wensley-Pritchard's estate, including the village, etc., has been bought by the man I work for.'

'He now owns the whole bang shoot?'

Claire nodded. 'He completed the deal last week. But now that I know how you feel . . .'

'Hang on!' Stephanie said quickly. 'I may have my own personal views about the remnants of the old British feudal system, but I don't go around shoving them down everyone's throat, you know. Does this boss of yours, who apparently now owns the village, intend to live here?'

'Yes, I think so. Apparently, it turns out that his family used to own the estate about two hundred years ago. So that makes it a bit better, doesn't it?' Claire added with a pleading note in her voice.

'Sure it does,' Stephanie agreed soothingly, gazing at the younger girl's flushed cheeks, and the agitated fingers plucking nervously at her woollen skirt. 'And this man? Is he sort of important to you, too—*personally* important, I mean?'

The girl's embarrassed nod only confirmed what she had already begun to suspect about the situation. There had been one or two casual boyfriends when Claire was studying at university, of course, but it very much looked as if her stepdaughter had now, for the very first time, fallen deeply in love. Stephanie couldn't help wishing that the girl had chosen someone nearer her own age. It didn't sound as though a businessman—who could afford to shell out the millions necessary to buy the estate—was likely to be in the first flush of youth. However, it was obviously vital that she should play her part, and help matters along as best she could.

'There's no need for you to worry about a thing,' she assured the girl with a warm smile. 'I'll be pleased to see this guy and, what's more, I promise not to give him an earful about my revolutionary ideals. OK?'

She was rewarded by the glowing, radiant happiness which swept over Claire's face as she rushed over to give her stepmother a hug, before almost dancing out of the room to make a long private telephone call.

It had been a busy week in her knitwear shop, and Stephanie had almost forgotten that Claire's new boyfriend—who also seemed to be that rarefied creature, a Lord of the Manor—was due to call on Saturday. Not that she'd really forgotten, of course, it was just that it had been all a bit of a rush to do the weekend shopping, pick up Adam from his school, and be back in time to welcome their visitor.

'Oh, good, they haven't turned up yet,' she muttered as she arrived back at the house. 'OK, out you get, Adam, and for heaven's sake, when you change out of that uniform do please put on a pair of clean jeans.'

'Is that strictly necessary?' the small, dark-haired boy enquired solemnly. 'I really can't believe that the course of true love will be affected one iota by any sartorial effort on my part. By the way, what's the name of Claire's boyfriend?'

'I don't know, darling. She quite obviously didn't want to talk about it, and so I thought best not to pry. We'll find out soon enough, in any case. But she's bound to be feeling a bit sensitive, so don't you dare mention one word about ''true love''!'

'That's two words,' he corrected her with a grin.

'You're so sharp, you'll cut yourself one of

these days,' she told him grimly, trying not to laugh.

'Relax, Mama. I promise you that I shall be the very soul of discretion,' he promised, picking up his case and leaping up the stairs two at a time.

'Just make sure that you behave yourself,' she called after him, knowing very well as she carried the shopping into the kitchen that it was a waste of time trying to have the last word—especially since her son's vocabulary was already larger than her own!

Becoming immersed in making a lasagne for lunch, and a large chocolate cake for Adam's tea, she hadn't realised how much time had gone by, until he came rushing into the room.

'I say, there's a brand new, fantastic-looking red Ferrari *Testarossa* pulling up outside,' he announced. 'It looks as if Claire's boyfriend has pots of money—do you think he might buy me a new computer?'

'No, of course he won't, she muttered, ripping off her apron and quickly tucking a stray tendril of hair back into the knot on top of her head. 'Oh, lord, this kitchen is such a mess!'

'Keep your cool,' advised her son. 'Claire and her boyfriend will undoubtedly—as they say in romantic novels—"only have eyes for each other".'

Stephanie snorted with dry amusement. 'Oh, yes—what would *you* know about romantic novels? I really don't understand you kids nowadays. When I was your age, I was still reading comics and children's books like, *What Katy Did*, she added, absent-mindedly slapping his hand as he dipped a finger in the chocolate icing.

'Honestly, Mother!' Adam shook his head sorrowfully. 'You're so out of date—positively antediluvian, in fact. Nowadays, it's much more likely to be "What Katy, Laura, Bob and Frank Did Behind the Cricket Pavillion"!' he grinned.

'*Adam!*'she gasped, prevented from saying any more as she heard the front door being opened. 'You and I are *definitely* going to have a few words later,' she told him sternly, before she hurried from the room.

'Ah, there you are,' Claire said as she entered the hall.

'Sorry, darling, I was busy getting lunch ready,' Stephanie murmured, turning with a welcoming smile to greet the tall figure of the man standing in the front doorway.

'I'd like to introduce you to my stepmother . . .' Claire began, but Stephanie wasn't listening. Frantically grabbing the back of a chair, her knuckles white with tension as she tried to prevent her legs from giving way beneath her, she was staring in stunned disbelief at Claire's 'boyfriend'.

As the blood drained from her face, her brain was hardly able to comprehend the dreadful, hideous fact that there—standing only a bare six feet away from her trembling figure—was Maxim Tyler!

CHAPTER TWO

MAXIM'S totally unexpected reappearance in her life had been, without the shadow of a doubt, one of the most cataclysmic and traumatic events she had ever experienced! Even now, a good two weeks later, Stephanie was still feeling tense and edgy, jumping nervously at shadows and quite convinced that every time she rounded a corner the dreaded man's malignant presence would, somehow, be there before her.

However, there was undoubtedly something very therapeutic about gardening. Leaning back on her heels, Stephanie raised a muddy, gloved hand to brush away some tendrils of hair which had fallen over her brow, and surveyed her progress with considerable satisfaction. The pale, early April sunlight was shining through the first new leaves on the trees, the birds were singing, and hacking viciously at the weeds in the herbaceous border was proving to be a splendid way of relieving her nervous tension.

'When are we having tea?'

She turned her head to see Adam leaning out of his bedroom window.

'We've only just had lunch, for heaven's sake!' she retorted with exasperation. There was no doubt that a boy's stomach seemed to be a

bottomless pit—keep tipping the food down and
they still yelled for more! All the same . . . 'OK, if
you're really hungry you can raid the biscuit tin,'
she called up to him, smiling as he gave a whoop
of delight and disappeared from view.

The smile slowly died from her face as she
turned back to stare blindly at a clump of yellow
daffodils. *What on earth was she going to do*? It was
a question she had been asking herself
practically every waking hour for the last four-
teen days—ever since Maxim Tyler had walked
so calmly and confidently into her house.

She simply hadn't been able to believe the
evidence of her own eyes. Gasping with horror,
all the breath driven from her body by the shock,
which had risen up to hit her like a hard blow to
the solar plexus, she had been totally unable to
believe that it really was Maxim, and not some
evil apparition or a figment of her imagination.

'Ah, Mrs Hammond, how nice to meet you,'
he had drawled, moving smoothly past her
trembling form and into the main body of the
hall.

Her vocal chords completely paralysed with
shock, Stephanie had stared at him with glazed
eyes, totally certain that she was in the midst of a
terrifying dream. She mustn't panic, she'd told
herself quickly, with the small part of her brain
which still seemed to be functioning. She must
keep absolutely calm and relaxed, because any
minute—pray God!—she was going to wake up
and discover that it was only a nightmare, after

all.

'What a charming house you have,' he continued, looking about him with interest. 'It is difficult to believe, from what your daughter has told me, that your home was once an old barn.'

'You're actually standing in one of the old cattle byres,' Claire told him with a laugh.

'Really?' he murmured, giving Stephanie a bland smile before turning his dark head to admire a picture on the wall.

'Oh, lord! *It really is Maxim*! Her trembling legs nearly collapsed as the dreadful truth began to slowly permeate the chaos in Stephanie's mind. The presence of this man, whom she had last seen ten years ago, and who had caused such unhappiness and pain in her life, wasn't a ghostly spectre or a phantom of her overheated imagination.

Recognition and fear welled up inside her, like a sudden sickness, her slim body beginning to shake as if in the fierce grip of a tropical fever. Gazing at him with horror-struck eyes, she realised that she had been quite right when she had felt certain that she must be in the throes of a bad dream. Unfortunately, the six foot, two inches of flesh, blood and sinew standing in the hall of her house, was an all too real, living nightmare that quite clearly wasn't going to go away.

'That's an old oil painting which my mother found in a junk shop,' Claire was explaining to Maxim. 'When it was cleaned, it turned out to be quite valuable. She's awfully good at finding things like that,' the girl added, smiling warmly at Stephanie's silent figure.

'Mmm . . . I'm sure she is,' Maxim drawled, bending closer to examine the brushwork.

She had to get out of here! Stephanie told herself frantically. Maxim didn't seem to have recognised her—not yet. She simply *must* have a few moments' peace and quiet to try and work out what was going on. Thankfully, it didn't seem as if Claire had noticed anything amiss —but that state of affairs wasn't going to last five seconds, not unless she could think of something—*anything!*—which would get this man out of the house. Luckily, the younger girl gave her the opening.

'Would you like a drink, or a cup of coffee?' Claire asked him.

'Coffee would be fine.'

'I . . er . .' Stephanie croaked, before clearing her voice and beginning again. 'I'll get it,' she said huskily, and, not giving either of them a chance to say anything, she practically ran into the kitchen.

Swiftly closing the door, she leaned back against it for a moment, gasping for breath. Her heart was pounding like a sledgehammer, just as if she had just been running a four-minute mile. And she really was in a race—a race against time, she thought, desperately trying to pull her shattered wits together. Because if she couldn't find a quick solution to the mess she was in, her

world was going to be blown up into smither-
eens, any minute now!

Quickly switching on the coffee percolator, she
glanced out through the kitchen window, and
saw that Adam was now busy tinkering with his
bicycle. She bit her lip with indecision, hesitating
for a moment before her attention was distracted
by the sound of voices coming from the next
room. Walking quietly across to the door which
led to the sitting-room, she peered through a
crack in the opening, and saw that Claire was
obviously giving Maxim a brief potted history of
the work involved in turning the barn into a
home.

'. . . and it took simply ages to clean up all the
beams,' the girl was saying. 'Some of them were
rotten, and my mother had to scour the
countryside before she found enough old timber
to match the ones up there,' Claire added,
pointing up to the ancient beams on the high
vaulted ceiling.

Stephanie couldn't hear any more as they
began walking to the other end of the room, but
in any case her whole attention was now focused
on the presence of the man talking to her stepdaughter.

Maxim Tyler was all that she had tried so hard
to forget—and more. The cliché, 'tall, dark and
handsome', might have been coined for his lean,
broad-shouldered figure as he moved lithely
around the room. Dark, he certainly was, with
his tanned olive skin and jet-black hair lying

thick and smooth over his well-shaped head,
before sweeping down to curl slightly over the
edge of his collar. He was maybe a little thinner
than she remembered, and although he must be
now about forty-one or two, only the silver
strands among the dark hair at his temples
hinted at the passage of the past ten years.

The devil looks after his own, she thought
grimly, moving slowly back across the kitchen to
get the cups and saucers out of the cupboard. It
was all so unfair! Why couldn't he have gone
bald? Or grown fat? Or . . . well, anything rather
than have remained the same diabolically
attractive man he had always been. No wonder
Claire had fallen for him like a ton of bricks.

At the thought of her darling stepdaughter's
involvement with Maxim, it was all Stephanie
could do not to groan out loud. She had no idea
of his life-style nowadays, of course. No way of
knowing if he was still married to his rich wife.
However, since his marriage vows hadn't
stopped him from playing around with other
women in the past, it wasn't likely that he had
suddenly become a reformed character, she
thought grimly. So, what about poor Claire? Did
she know that she was involved with a married
man?

Burying her face in her hands for a moment,
Stephanie fought to control the memory of the
pain and torment she had suffered because of
the man in the next room. She musn't—she
simply *musn't* let it happen to Claire.

But Maxim's present marital state was only one of the pressing questions that needed an answer, she realised, shaking her head distractedly as she tried to force her dazed mind to function normally.

There were many more—and all of them were equally frightful! For instance, how was Claire going to react when she discovered the past relationship between Maxim and herself?

The girl was, of course, a reasonably sophisticated twenty-one-year-old, but Stephanie very much doubted if she herself at that age would have been able to handle such a fraught situation. For Claire to learn that her stepmother had been involved in a torrid love-affair before she met and married James Hammond wasn't ideal—but neither was it an earth-shaking disaster. Young girls nowadays weren't wrapped in cotton wool, and could read about far worse things in the newspapers any day of the week. But what was going to happen . . . How was Claire going to feel when she found out that the man in her mother's past, was the very same Maxim Tyler with whom she was now so much in love?

Stephanie's legs nearly buckled beneath her, and she had to sit down quickly on a nearby chair as the full magnitude of the problem hit her with the force of a thunderclap. She was facing a total family disaster! Because having to cope with all the emotional and psychological overtones of *that* scenario was going to demand a degree of worldly finesse and sophistication which neither she nor Claire possessed.

On top of which . . . Stephanie shook her head distractedly as she tried to work out the permutations of the situation. In the end, she was forced to the conclusion that it all seemed to rest on whether or not Maxim had recognised her.

It was, of course, *just* marginally possible that Maxim didn't know who she was. Trying to recall the brief conversation in the dark, shadowy hall, she was sure that Claire hadn't called her by her Christian name. And there was the chance that, while their affair had been such a traumatic event in her life, she might well have been only one of a long string of conquests, most of whom Maxim would have now forgotten.

However, if he *had* recognised her, why was he acting as though she was a complete stranger? It simply didn't make any sense. Not unless——? Could it be that setting eyes on her had been every bit as upsetting for Maxim as for herself? She hadn't noticed any sign of shock on his part, but she hadn't been in a fit state to notice anything; and it might be that he had better control over his emotions. Maybe he, too, feared the exposure of their past relationship? And he would, therefore, take very good care not to hurt Claire. Right?

For the first time since Maxim's dramatic reappearance in her life, Stephanie felt a faint flicker of hope. She still had another major problem to contend with, of course. But if, as now seemed likely, the dreadful man was likely to leave as soon as he decently could, well . . .

'Stephanie?' Claire's voice from behind startled her. 'How's the coffee coming along?'

'Oh, fine—it's almost ready,' she muttered breathlessly as she leaped to her feet, overwhelmingly relieved to see that Maxim hadn't accompanied Claire into the kitchen. She threw a nervous smile at the girl. 'Why don't you take the tray in? I'm awfully busy today. I've . . . er . . . I've still got some shopping to do,' Stephanie added, improvising wildly. 'Besides, I'm sure that you and Mr Tyler will have a lot to talk about, so you don't need me hanging around.'

'What nonsense,' Claire said with a laugh. 'Of course I want you "hanging around", as you put it. Why this sudden shrinking violet act? Or . . . or is it that you don't like the look of him?' she asked anxiously.

You're so right—I don't! Stephanie thought hysterically. 'Oh, yes, he seems . . . er . . . very nice,' she mumbled helplessly as she picked up the tray.

It didn't seem as if she had any alternative. She was going to have to face Maxim again, and with a stomach which seemed to be churning nervously around like a cement mixer she braced herself for the forthcoming ordeal.

'I've been admiring your décor, Mrs Hammond,' Maxim drawled as she entered the room. 'It's certainly very unusual.'

'I'm glad you like it,' she muttered, keeping her back to him as she concentrated on pouring the coffee.

'I was wondering what led you to choose such a style?' He paused, and when she didn't immediately reply Claire leaped into the silence.

'Oh, it was all due to a lack of money, wasn't it?' she said with a nervous laugh, glancing apprehensively at Stephanie's silent figure.

'Yes, I . . .' There was nothing for it. She was going to have to go through the polite motions of this conversation—if only for her stepdaughter's sake. 'Claire's quite right,' she said, slowly turning around to face him. 'Converting this house took most of the money I had at the time, and so I decided to decorate the room as it would have been in Tudor times, when the barn was originally built. It also had the merit of being a cheap option,' she added, deliberately not looking at him as she glanced around at her surroundings.

She really ought to do the whole place over, she thought, suddenly seeing the room through his eyes. The cold, early spring sunlight pouring in through the large window was cruelly illuminating the threadbare tapestries hanging on the wall. The severity of the heavy oak tables and high-backed, tall chairs was relieved by piles of large silk cushions, but there was no denying that the wide oak-beamed, highly polished floor wasn't half as comfortable as a proper carpet

would have been. And maybe she had rather
gone over the top with some of her ideas—like
mounds of creamy-white wax cascading down
from the giant candles which could only be
bought from a clerical supply shop in London.
She had been so thrilled to have found the huge,
five-foot high carved wooden gilt candlesticks,
rescuing them from a redundant church in the
nick of time before they were put on a bonfire.
And to sit in this room at night, warming herself
by a roaring log fire as she listened to music by
candlelight, was one of the great pleasures of her
life.

However, she had no illusions. She knew that
the room must look very tawdry to an outsider;
and especially to a man who had just spent
goodness knows how many millions buying up
the whole village. Well—to hell with him! There
were a lot of things which were far more
important than a whole heap of money.

'Claire tells me that you've bought old Mrs
Wensley-Pritchard's estate,' she said
breathlessly, her pulse quickening as Maxim
came over to take the cup and saucer from her
hand.

'Yes.' He gazed down at her with a cool smile,
which held not a trace of recognition. 'My
ancestors used to own the estate, way back in
the eighteenth century. My side of the family is
descended from a younger son, who emigrated
to the States quite a few generations ago. And
so, when I heard it was up for sale . . .' He

shrugged.

'You decided to buy it back,' she said, beginning to feel slightly more confident. It really was beginning to look—however unlikely it might seem—that he had no memory of their previous association. 'Are you intending to live here, in the village?'

'Oh, yes, indeed I am. The builders will be starting work on the alterations to the manor house next week.'

She knew that she ought to stop there. She had, after all, promised Claire that she wouldn't upset the apple-cart. But that was before she knew this loathsome man—any day now—was going to be living only five hundred yards away from her own home.

'I was wondering how you, as an American, feel about becoming a feudal landlord?' she asked.

He frowned as he caught the caustic tone in her voice. 'I don't exactly envisage . . .'

'Oh, goodness, your coffee must be cold,' Claire said swiftly, in an obvious attempt to distract his attention from the potentially difficult, awkward subject. Giving Stephanie a frowning, reproachful look, she quickly took the cup from his hand. 'I'll get you some more from the kitchen.'

Don't leave me alone with him! Stephanie wanted to scream as the girl hurried from the room. And it was no comfort to realise, as she turned away to fiddle nervously with an arrangement of dried flowers on the table beside her, that she had only herself to blame for Claire's absence.

'Do I take it, Mrs Hammond, that you don't approve of my purchase of the estate?'

The dry note of amusement in his voice was distinctly unnerving, and she tensed as he took a step nearer.

'I . . . er . . . it's nothing to do with me,' she muttered wildly, the close proximity of his tall figure sending a sudden, sharp quiver of sexual awareness scorching through her body.

Closing her eyes for a moment, she took a shaky, unsteady breath as she tried, with every force at her command, *not* to allow herself to recall the broad shoulders, slim hips and firmly muscled thighs which lay beneath the dark grey, immaculately tailored suit he was wearing with such ease and assurance.

'Well, now, Mrs Hammond,' he purred softly, 'I'm *very* sorry to hear you say that. Especially since we're now going to be such *close* neighbours.'

She gasped, her eyes flying to his face as she immediately realised from the dark, sardonic mockery with which he had emphasised his last few words that he *had* recognised her, after all.

'You . . . you know, don't you?' she whispered.

' "Know", Mrs Hammond?' He raised a dark, satanic eyebrow as he looked at her with a bland, cool smile on his lips. 'I know many things. What particular subject did you have in mind?'

He hadn't changed, she thought, suddenly feeling totally exhausted and sick to death of the whole ghastly charade. He had always been known for conducting his financial and business affairs with a skill that was thoroughly Machiavellian. And she only had to recall Harold's words the other day to realise that Maxim had merely refined his technique over the years.

Well, he wasn't going to play games with *her*, she told herself, a deep tide of anger flowing through her veins. It might well be that her safe, secure world was going to disintegrate at any moment, but to be forced to dance on the end of a string manipulated by this man—that would be a far worse fate!

'OK, Maxim, there's no need to go through the whole, "surprise, surprise—guess who's here?" scene with me,' she told him in a low, savage tone. 'I don't know what you hope to achieve by this nonsense—and I don't care.'

He stood staring down at her in silence. His face was devoid of all expression, only a slight clenching of his jaw betraying any tension.

'You've had your coffee,' she continued bitterly. 'Now I want you to leave, and . . .' She broke off hurriedly as Claire came back into the room.

'I'm sorry I was so long,' the girl said, not seeming to notice the strained atmosphere between their two rigidly stiff figures as she handed Maxim a cup and saucer. 'I got side-tracked by Adam, who wanted to try out a new opening in chess. Needless to say, the horrid boy had me checkmated before I'd moved more than a couple of pieces!' She laughed.

Stephanie's eyes flew towards the door which led to the kitchen. *Oh, no!* But there was nothing she could do as she saw that Adam, with the chessboard in his hand, was already walking towards them.

'I wonder whether you would care for a game?' he asked Maxim.

'I really don't think . . .' Claire began.

'I'm sure he'd love a game of chess, darling,' Stephanie said quickly. 'But . . . um . . . unfortunately Mr Tyler is just leaving. So why don't you go upstairs and mess around with your computer?' she added, a note of urgency in her voice as Maxim put down his cup on the table, and turned towards the boy.

'I'm afraid that I don't have the time,' he began pleasantly, glancing idly at the boy from beneath his heavy lids.

'But I know you do play chess.' Adam grinned up at the man. 'I hope you don't mind, but I looked inside your car, and there was a small travel set on the dashboard. I must say,' he added reflectively, 'that from the way you'd left the pieces, it looks as if you've thoroughly messed up that Ruy Lopez opening.'

'Have I now?' Maxim murmured, his dark

eyebrows drawing together in an abstracted frown as he stared down at the boy.

Stephanie held her breath, frightened that if she so much as moved a muscle she would somehow precipitate the next act of the domestic tragedy which she could see no way of avoiding. Claire was so used to her brother that she might not notice. But a perceptive man like Maxim?

Her glance flicked between the two dark heads which, despite the distance in height between them, bore the same blue-black sheen, the colour of raven's wings. And the eyes . . . the same gold flecks shimmering in the emerald green eyes beneath their heavy lids; surely Maxim couldn't fail to make the connection?

'Do you play a lot of chess?' Maxim asked quietly.

Adam shrugged. 'A reasonable amount. Unfortunately, it's becoming increasingly difficult to find worthy opponents. I'm really not trying to boast, or be big-headed,' the boy added quickly. 'But if you play the game, you'll appreciate the essential requisite, which is to measure one's abilities against those of a player of the same standard.'

Maxim looked stunned. As he continued to stare silently down at Adam, Stephanie at last managed to break out of her mental strait-jacket.

'I—er—I'm quite sure the last thing Mr Tyler wants is a lecture,' she said breathlessly, trying to head off disaster. 'And since he's undoubtedly a very busy man, we really mustn't keep him any further.'

'Yes, I must be off,' Maxim said slowly, his eyes still fixed on the boy. 'Just before we go . . .' He paused. 'Do you mind telling me how old you are?'

'Nine . . . going on one hundred and two!' Claire answered with a laugh, before Adam could reply. 'But Stephanie's right. We really ought to go and look around the village. It gets dark so early at this time of year, and you've got a lot of people to see.'

'You're quite right, Claire, as always,' he said, giving the girl a warm smile, before turning back to Stephanie's trembling figure.

'It's been very interesting meeting you, Mrs Hammond,' he drawled smoothly, his eyes flicking briefly down at her son for a moment. 'Quite—quite revealing, one might even say, hmm?'

'Goodbye, Mr Tyler,' she muttered dully, her mind filled with the bleak, sombre knowledge that she wasn't going to be seeing the last of him.

'I'm sorry I have to go now,' he told Adam, before confirming her worst fears as he raised his head, his green eyes raking her pale face with chilling intensity. 'But I'll be back,' he added, his words echoing in her ears like the knell of doom. 'I shall return very soon, that I promise you!'

And he would return, of that she had absolutely no doubt, Stephanie told herself grimly as she got to her feet, and put the last clump of weeds into the wheelbarrow. It was just a case of *when*.

She'd never been through such a fraught, nervously exhausting time as she had during the last two weeks. Expecting Maxim to suddenly materialise any minute, like the evil magician in a pantomime, meant that she hadn't been able to relax for one minute. She couldn't rest, she couldn't sleep, and all the stress and strain of the last fortnight had taken a considerable toll; looking in the mirror each morning after yet another sleepless night had been a truly horrible experience. It was difficult to believe that the pale, strained face with those dark shadows beneath the haunted blue eyes really belonged to her. Even Lisa, her assistant in the shop, had been shocked by her appearance.

'You're not looking too good,' she had said with concern as they had checked the stock a few days ago. 'Why not take some time off? I can easily cope with everything we've got on at the moment.'

It had been kind of her, Stephanie told herself as she gathered the gardening tools together, and carried them over to a shed at the back of the barn. But it wasn't the answer. Just as her wild thoughts of grabbing Adam and running away to another country had, in the cold light of day, proved to be hopelessly impracticable.

She knew she ought to be doing something, but she seemed to be paralysed by indecision. Of course, the whole terrible mess wasn't *all*

Maxim's fault. Maybe, if she hadn't been so young, or had had more experience of the world, it might have occurred to her that such an attractive and handsome man, so much older than herself, was also likely to be a married man. However, at only nineteen years of age she had been still pathetically naïve and wet between the ears when she had been invited to that charity reception in New York—a far more glamorous affair than anything she had ever attended before. And if Mrs Blair, the chairman of the charity committee, hadn't been so insistent, she would never have gone. But the older woman had been so delighted with the prize-winning design for the charity poster which Stephanie had submitted in order to earn a few extra dollars that she had pressed the young art student to attend.

So she'd plucked up her nerve and attended the party at Mrs Blair's prestigious apartment block on East 86th Street. And . . . well, that had been it, really. It truly had been one of those 'eyes meeting across a crowded room' love stories, which had inspired so many romantic songs and novels, but which never seemed to happen in real life. Except that it *had* happened to her. One moment she had been standing at the side of the room, nervously clutching a glass in her hand—and when she'd next come back down to earth she was being swept out to dinner by the most devastatingly attractive man she had ever seen.

Oh, if only she hadn't been so young! Stephanie cringed now as she looked back at her younger self, and remembered how there had scarcely been a heartbeat between setting eyes on the sophisticated businessman and falling deeply and irrevocably in love with him. He had escorted her back to the small apartment which she'd bought with the inheritance left to her by her parents following their death in an air crash—and, once inside the door, he had swept her up in his arms and carried her into the bedroom.

Stephanie had never known such happiness. It was as if she and Maxim had existed in a small, completely separate world which contained only themselves and their love for each other; a halcyon time of intense rapture and overwhelming passion—which in her youth and folly she had believed would last for ever.

Even now, after all these years, she found it almost impossible to realise that their love affair had been of such brief duration—a mere five days. But Stephanie could still remember every second, minute and hour of that precious time when they had been so completely absorbed with one other. Above all, she had been totally secure in the knowledge that he did, as he frequently assured her, love her with every fibre of his being. Until that dreadful moment when she had awoken in the middle of the night to find him fully dressed and pacing the floor with a hard, grim expression on his face.

'It's all over, Stephanie,' he had said heavily, coming over to sit down on the bed beside her. 'I'm sorry, darling—but there's no prospect of us ever being able to have a permanent relationship together—either now or in the future. So it's best if I terminate matters right now. Clear out, and not come back.'

Only being half awake, she had protested, muttering something about it being a bad joke at that time of night, and then her blood had run cold, freezing in her veins as he proceeded to ruthlessly smash her love and her dreams into little pieces.

'The fact is—it's the old, old story: I'm a married man,' he had confessed with a heavy sigh. 'Estelle was a widow when I married her, with a small boy who is now thirteen—just six years younger than yourself. I guess that makes me quite a cradle-snatcher as far as you're concerned, doesn't it?' His voice had been harsh with self-contempt. 'While my wife is obviously some years older than I am, that's no excuse for the hurt I'm likely to cause her—or you. Believe me, there's nothing that you can say which will make me feel any worse than I do already,' he'd added grimly as she stared at him with horrified eyes.

'But . . . Maxim—you can't do this to me!'

'I'm desperately sorry, darling. I . . . well, I guess it's as though I've fallen into some extraordinary kind of time-warp these past few days.' He had pushed a shaking hand through his black hair. 'But I've managed to pull myself together, and I now see that I've been behaving in a thoroughly irresponsible and reckless manner. So I'm leaving you now—while I can still do so.'

Despite her tearful, almost hysterical protests, he had remained adamant. Quickly picking up his briefcase, he had moved towards the door of her small apartment. 'You're so young, Stephanie, and you have your whole life in front of you,' he'd said with a tired, weary smile. 'You won't believe me now, but you'll soon get over this small hiccup. It won't be long before you'll be thanking your lucky stars—and eternally grateful to me for having the sense to walk away.'

The door had closed behind his tall figure, and the last she had heard of him was the faint, indistinct clatter of his leather shoes on the stone steps. And then there had been nothing but silence.

Completely devastated by his sudden departure, it had been some agonising, wretchedly unhappy weeks later before she discovered that she was expecting a baby . . .

'Mother?'

Stephanie looked up, startled to find her son standing before her.

'I've been hunting for you everywhere. What on earth are you doing—sitting in a wheelbarrow, here in the potting shed?' he asked with a grin.

'Oh, I was . . . I was just thinking,' she

muttered, standing up and brushing the earth and bits of twigs from her jeans.

'Well, I do hope that you haven't forgotten the *very* important fact that you've promised to take me and my friend Oliver to the new James Bond movie—or that we're going to that new hamburger restaurant afterwards.'

'No, of course I haven't. Run along and get changed, and then we'll be off, OK?'

'Super!' he said, giving a jump of excitement before racing back to the house.

Smiling wryly, Stephanie finished tidying away the tools. Adam might be a very clever little boy, but despite all that brain-power he still enjoyed exactly the same pastimes as other children of his own age.

What would Maxim make of his son? she wondered. And more to the point—how, if he ever found out the truth, would Adam react to the news that James Hammond wasn't his real father?

Sighing heavily, Stephanie left the shed and walked slowly back across the garden towards the house. If only she could talk to someone about the situation. But unless they knew Maxim as well as she did, none of her friends would have considered that she had any problem at all. After all, she wasn't the first young girl—and she certainly wouldn't be the last—to have become pregnant by a married man. And the fact that she hadn't known, until it was far too late, that he had a wife—well, that wasn't an unusual story, either. So why all the panic?

Maxim Tyler, that was the simple answer. She'd known immediately what Harold had meant when he'd said, that what Maxim Tyler wanted, he got! He'd clearly been shattered by the realisation that he had a son, and just as clearly she had sensed his deep, burning anger that the knowledge had been kept from him. Would he now decide that he wanted Adam? She had no idea about the legal position; but even if she had the law one hundred per cent on her side that wouldn't stop Maxim from keeping her tied up in the courts until doomsday. Not to mention all the attendant publicity. He'd know that she wouldn't be able to face that, or to allow it to affect her son. Or Claire, for that matter.

At the thought of the dreadful, ghastly triangle in which she and her stepdaughter appeared to be enmeshed, Stephanie nearly whimpered aloud. Whichever way she looked, it seemed as though she was trapped in a hopelessly confusing maze from which there was no possible exit. In fact, there was only one thing about which she *was* certain. Maxim was not the man to make idle threats. She had no way of knowing either the day or the time, but when he had said he would return—she had absolutely no doubt that he would do so.

CHAPTER THREE

'WELL, we seem to have tied up everything as far as your accounts are concerned. How did you get on at the Designer Show at Olympia? Was it busy?'

'Hectic!' Stephanie grinned at her accountant. 'However, apart from buying stock for the shop, I also managed to double the sales of my own designs from last year—which is really great. The Spinning Wheel label seems to be doing really very well, both here and in the States.'

Guy Fletcher smiled. 'I've never had a client in the fashion business before. I've often wondered how you came to choose that name for the shop and the business.'

'Everyone I knew came up with so many suggestions that I nearly went mad!' She grinned. 'In the end, I decided that it seemed to be the most appropriate, somehow. Although I must admit that I was tempted to use Claire's suggestion: Ewe-Too!' She laughed at his wry grimace. 'Or some of the other ideas floating around at the time. How do Knit-Knax, Wool-gathering or Ewe-phoria grab you?'

'They don't!' He shuddered.

'Anyway, the name isn't important. The only

thing that really matters is that I seem to be making a good profit,' she added firmly. 'Especially since it means I'll now be able to afford to pay your monumentally high fees!'

'*Stephanie*, how can you say that?' Guy looked at her with a wounded expression. 'You know how I feel about you. If you would just . . .'

'I was only joking,' she said quickly, turning her head to smile gratefully up at the waiter who was pouring her another cup of coffee. The last thing she felt she could cope with at the moment was yet another proposal of marriage from Guy.

She ought to be ashamed of herself, Stephanie thought guiltily. Right from the first day she'd walked into the offices of Fletcher & Co., she had known that Guy Fletcher was just as interested in her personally as he was in the accountancy and tax affairs of her business. And when he had, over the past few years, made his intentions towards her as clear as daylight, she really should have been far more discouraging.

Unfortunately, Guy's professional expertise and guidance had proved to be so helpful and constructive that she was reluctant to give up his services. 'And why should you?' her assistant Lisa had exclaimed with surprise. 'Honestly, love, I think you must be out of your mind! He's well off, very good-looking, and he's crazy about you—what more do you want? If you've got any sense, you'll grab him while you've got the chance!'

And Lisa was right, she mused, looking at

Guy as he settled the bill. He really did have just
about everything going for him. Tall, with fair
hair and blue eyes, he was also one of the
kindest and most considerate men she had ever
met. Now a senior partner in the family firm
which had been founded by his grandfather, his
parents were a very sweet couple, who had
made it abundantly clear that they hoped she
would become their son's wife. But Stephanie,
who had once so long ago—however briefly—
experienced paradise in another man's arms,
had always known that despite all his virtues
Guy Fletcher was not the man for her.

'By the way,' Guy's words broke into her
thoughts, 'I managed to get two tickets for that
concert in Cheltenham next week. You
remember?' he added, when she looked at him
blankly. 'You said that you'd heard a rumour
that they were all sold out.'

'Oh, yes—yes, of course,' she murmured, her
heart sinking. Why on earth hadn't she kept her
mouth shut? She might have known that Guy
would have picked up her brief reference to the
concert.

He looked at her anxiously. 'You do still want
to go, don't you?'

'Hmm . . . yes, it will be great fun. It was very
kind of you to . . . Oh, good heavens—just look
at the time!' she exclaimed quickly. 'Lisa wants
to go off early today, so I really must get back to
the shop. It's been a lovely meal,' she added,
giving him a warm smile, slightly tinged with

guilt. 'In fact, the only drawback to being wined and dined in the middle of the day is in having to return to work for the rest of the afternoon.'

'I'll walk you back to the shop,' he said as she bent down to pick up her bag from beside her chair.

'There's no need . . .'

'I insist,' he said firmly, helping her on with her coat and taking her arm as they left the restaurant.

Maybe Lisa had a point, Stephanie thought, gasping as the full force of the cold air nearly took her breath away. It *was* pleasant to have the comfort of a man's strong presence shielding her from the worst of the blustery wind, and helping her avoid the puddles from last night's rain-storm. Not enough to make it a permanent arrangement—such as getting married, for instance, but still . . .

Oh, come on—get a grip on yourself, and stop being so damn silly! she told her inner self roughly. The very last thing she wanted was any more complications in her life, and if she hadn't let Guy persuade her into having some wine with their meal she wouldn't be allowing herself to even entertain such foolish ideas. Alcohol was definitely a trap for the unwary, she thought grimly. But after the fraught tension of the last three weeks she had begun to hope that she might at last be able to relax.

Despite having been so certain that Maxim would seek her out, she was now beginning to think that she could have been mistaken. After all, it wasn't beyond the realms of possibility that Maxim *might* have changed over the last ten years—unlikely, of course, but not totally out of the question. And, after what Tilly had said, maybe there had been no need for all that panic-stricken, wild despair and torment, which had left her feeling so shattered?

It had run like wildfire through the village, of course. Stow-under-Hill was now buzzing with the news that both the Lordship of the Manor, and the estate, had been bought by a rich American businessman whose family had owned it in the dim and distant past. In fact, she thought sourly, if her housekeeper's enthusiastic response was anything to go by, it looked as if the PR department of Maxim's company was definitely working overtime.

'That Mr Tyler's got the builders in at the manor house already,' Tilly had announced at the beginning of last week. 'Goodness knows what it's all going to cost, first to last, but it's as plain as the nose on my face that he's not short of a bob or two! Tom Watson at the Cross Keys says he's heard that it's a real case of "money no object"! And seeing as how all the cottages are going to be repainted, and the estate office is busy stocking the farms with new machinery, I reckon that old Tom is right,' she'd added, her cheeks pink with excitement. 'Oh, I tell you, Mrs Hammond, it's the best news we've had in this village since . . . well, I don't know when!'

Tilly's only disappointment, since all arrangements had been handled so far by a large, well-known firm of land agents, was that nobody had actually seen the new Lord of the Manor. 'Not that he's a *real* lord, of course,' she had said with a sigh of regret. 'Still, even if he hardly ever comes here, that don't matter. It's keeping the village like it always has been—that's what counts, isn't it?'

After listening to her housekeeper's gossip, Stephanie was rapidly coming to the conclusion that she might have been foolish to have over-reacted in the way she had. Especially since it now seemed as though Maxim was going to be an absentee landlord. And so, although she wasn't entirely convinced that she had seen the last of him, the continuing silence and non-appearance of the man who had so dramatically invaded her life had led to a gradual lessening of her nervous stress and tension.

The fact that the past few days had been very hectic ones had also helped, of course. However, now that she'd had such a success with her designs at Olympia during the British Fashion and Design Show, she was going to have to get her merry band of knitters going, she reminded herself as Guy turned into the arcade which led to her shop. She was very lucky in having managed to find so many superb handknitters living locally, who ranged in age from eighteen to eighty. However, their needles would really have to start clicking with a vengeance, particularly if she was hoping to fulfil all her orders on time.

'Here you are.'

'Hmm . . . ?' She looked up to see they were outside the shop. 'Thank you for the lunch, Guy—and for getting hold of the concert tickets. You're altogether much too good to me,' she told him, before reaching up to give him a brief kiss on the cheek.

'Named the day yet?' Lisa enquired as she entered the shop.

'Oh, for heaven's sake!' Stephanie groaned, her cheeks flushing slightly beneath her assistant's wide, cynical grin. If people were now beginning to think of Guy and herself as a couple well on the way to the altar, maybe she really *was* going to have to get a new accountant! 'OK, Lisa, if you think he's so gorgeous—why don't *you* try batting your long eyelashes at him?'

'With you around? I should get so lucky!'

Lisa sighed, gazing at the other girl, who was wearing a tightly fitting, soft lambswool dress which clung to the curves of her slim figure. She must remember that envy was one of the seven deadly sins, Lisa told herself glumly. Nobody who was even a few pounds overweight could wear one of those dresses, and that particular shade of crushed raspberry would normally be the kiss of death on anyone with ash-blonde hair. But there certainly wasn't any justice in the world, because although she obviously hadn't been too well during the past few weeks, Stephanie was now looking fantastic!

Shrugging her shoulders, Lisa gave a dry laugh, and pointed to her ample curves. 'I'm going to have to face it—after the divorce, and the past two years of "comfort" eating, my eyelashes may be in great shape, but I've still got to beat the battle of the bulge!'

'All you need is motivation. You can do it,' Stephanie murmured encouragingly as she went over to check the till. 'What's the diet this week?'

'Grilled liver and orange juice.'

'Ugh!'

Lisa grinned. 'You're right—it's awful. To tell the truth, I'm not sure *any* man is worth eating that for, but . . . Oh, lord, I nearly forgot! Talking of gorgeous men, there's one waiting for you upstairs.'

'In the apartment?' Stephanie raised an eyebrow in surprise. 'Who is it?'

'I don't know, love,' the other woman said with a shrug of her shoulders. 'He wouldn't give his name, but as he mentioned that he had a large order to give you, I didn't like to tell him to go away, and come back another day. Besides, I couldn't have him standing around down here all afternoon, could I? He's a very—er—very *masculine* type of man, if you know what I mean?'

Stephanie looked at her with a puzzled frown. 'Not really, no.'

'Well, I'd just about sold that hideously expensive, pink cashmere number to little Miss

Wallace, when she caught sight of this chap
looming over her—and promptly scuttled from
the shop. That sort of thing is definitely *not* good
for trade,' Lisa added firmly.

'No, I can see it's not,' Stephanie agreed. 'OK,
I'd better go and see who it is and what he
wants.'

She had just opened the door at the rear of the
shop and was beginning to mount the steps to
the small apartment above when Lisa called out,
'Oh, I forgot to mention that I think he's an
American. Or he could be Canadian, of course. I
can never tell the difference,' she added with a
laugh, as the doorbell tinkled, and a customer
came into the shop.

Stephanie paused, taking a deep breath before
she continued walking up the stairs. Pull yourself together, she lectured herself grimly.
Practically having heart failure because an
unknown man wanted to see her wasn't just
stupid—it was plainly ridiculous. In fact, if she
didn't watch out, she was going to find herself
with a terminal case of persecution mania!

However, as she entered the small apartment
and closed the door behind her, Stephanie
discovered that her sixth sense hadn't let her
down; all her dark, gloomy premonitions had
been fully justified.

Following the unrelenting tension and fear of
the past days and weeks, to at last find herself
face to face with the man who had so haunted
her dreams now came almost as a relief,

she realised, gazing across the dimly lit room at the tall outline of the figure standing by her desk at the window.

'What are you doing here, Maxim?' she asked, in as firm a tone as she could manage.

'You know very well why I'm here,' he drawled.

'My assistant told me you wished to place a large order with my business,' she replied evenly, determined not to give an inch.

Used primarily as an office, the two-roomed apartment with its tiny bathroom and kitchen was admittedly very small. But now it contained both Maxim's tall figure and the dominant, powerful force of his strong personality, it seemed minuscule. Daylight was fading outside in the arcade, and the light from a small lamp on a nearby table barely illuminated the far corners of the room, throwing dark shadows across his face as he turned slowly to face her.

'Why didn't you tell me?'

'Tell you what?'

Maxim frowned impatiently, raising his hand for a moment in a gesture of irritation. 'Why didn't you tell me that Adam was my son?'

'That . . . that's nonsense,' she said huskily. 'Where on earth did you get such a ridiculous idea?'

'Don't try and play games with me, Stephanie,' he retorted curtly, his hard green eyes beneath their heavy lids riveted on her pale face. 'I want to know why you never told me that you were expecting my child?'

'Good heavens—why on earth should I make up a story like that?' She gave a shrill, high-pitched laugh.

His lips tightened ominously. 'Because it's the truth. And because I had a right to know,' he said harshly.

'You had—and have—no "rights" as far as I and my son are concerned,' she retorted, raising her chin defiantly. 'I'm not denying that you and I had a brief affair—but so what?' She shrugged. 'You went back to your wife, and I came to England and married James Hammond—end of story.'

'But it wasn't the end of the story, was it?' he drawled with grim, silky menace as he began moving slowly across the carpet towards her.

'Yes, of course it was,' she muttered, bitterly aware of the hot colour flooding her cheeks. She had never been any good at telling lies, but in this case she had no choice, she told herself desperately. No choice at all.

'You were pregnant with my child before you left the States . . .'

'No!'

'And you married that man, Hammond, purely to give your—*my*—child a father,' he continued remorselessly, the flat, hard certainty in his voice echoing in her ears like a death knell as she backed nervously away from his tall figure.

The tension in the small room was so thick and claustrophobic, she could almost cut it with a knife, she thought hysterically, her heart pounding and thumping like a kettledrum as Maxim stood staring grimly down at her. The expression on his face made shivers of sick fear run down her back, warning her, if she had needed any such reminder, of the extreme folly in defying this seemingly invincible man.

Calling on all her reserves of strength, she took a deep breath. 'You're wrong,' she croaked, flinching at the blaze of anger which flared in his eyes. 'Adam is *not* your son . . .' she added desperately, her progress backwards abruptly halted as she felt her spine jar on the wall behind her.

'Don't lie to me!' he grated, and she gasped as his hand suddenly took hold of her chin, forcing her head up towards him.

His cold green eyes bored into hers, and she felt as though her mind was being probed by a sharp, icy-cold scalpel. He was standing so close to her that she could see the faint flush of anger beneath his tanned skin, stretched tightly over his high cheekbones and formidable jawline; the cruel sensuality of his lips.

'There is no point in lying to me,' he said, his voice heavy with menace. 'I *know* Adam is my son.'

'But . . . but you can't know—not for certain,' she whispered, her eyes shifting warily beneath his fierce gaze as he leaned forward and she felt his long, muscular thigh touching her own.

Despite her fear of this dangerous man, and

desperately anxious to protect both herself and
her son, there was little she could do to prevent a
tremor of sexual response from quivering
through her trembling body. A pulse throbbed
frantically in her throat and she swallowed hard,
shutting her eyes tightly for a moment.

'Please . . . don't, Maxim,' she begged huskily,
her breath quickening as his hand began to move
slowly down the long line of her neck. Heat
scorched through her veins, the colour draining
from her face at the soft, velvet touch of his
fingers slipping erotically over her skin.

The silence lengthened between them in the
still, quiet room, the tension mounting second
by second until Stephanie could almost feel it
hammering inside her skull. She tried to tear her
eyes away, but they remained locked by the
intense, searching, almost hypnotic stare with
which he seemed to be invading her very soul.
Her senses violently disrupted by the close
proximity of his dark, satanic figure, it felt as if
she was drowning—conscious only of the
gleaming, topaz flecks in his darkening green
eyes as he slowly lowered his gaze towards her
trembling mouth.

Stephanie couldn't speak. She was suddenly
breathless, her whole body burning with a
frantic heat. There seemed nothing she could do
to break the spell holding her mentally
paralysed, like a wild beast trapped in the glare
of a car's headlamps; nothing she could do to
make her lips move, or release the tongue frozen

still in her mouth. She knew he was going to kiss her. She knew she must stop him, but there seemed no way to break free of the strange force which seemed to have her in thrall.

With slow, deliberate intent he lowered his head, and her nerves were almost at screaming pitch as his lips finally closed over her own. She was intensely conscious of the first, brief touch of his mouth, the aroma of his cologne and the warm, firm texture of his flesh on hers. And then, with a sudden, shocking movement, he quickly jerked her forward into his arms, which closed tightly about her as his kiss took on a new, demanding hunger she was powerless to resist.

She moaned helplessly beneath the ruthless heat of his mouth, the hard, firm contours of the body pressed too closely to her own. Shaken by frenzied shivers of excitement, she desperately tried to drag her rapidly dissolving mind back to some kind of sanity. She must . . . she *must* remember that this was the married man who had so cruelly and ruthlessly abandoned her, and for whom she wept such copious tears; the same man who was now—very possibly—romantically involved with her stepdaughter.

But it was such a long, long time since she had been held in his arms like this that there was little she could do to prevent all the barriers she had so carefully and deliberately erected over the years from being destroyed by the sweet seduction of his deepening kiss.

Drowning in a whirlpool of physical sensations, there seemed no strength she could summon to prevent her own senses from defeating her. She was aware only of deep, overwhelming desire, and a need so fierce and intense that it obliterated prudence and caution, leaving her helplessly trapped within the web of dark, sensual enchantment with which he held her, beyond free will and all common sense.

It was a long time before Maxim raised his head, his eyes glittering with aroused desire, his tanned face taut and strained as he stared down at her for a moment. And then, cursing fluently under his breath, he quickly let her go before he turned on his heel, walking slowly back across the floor to stare out of the window.

Trembling like a leaf, and shuddering from the storm of passion his lovemaking had released, Stephanie remained leaning helplessly against the wall for a moment. Her legs felt boneless, as if they could barely support her as she staggered towards a nearby armchair.

Collapsing into its soft depths, she desperately tried to control her shaking body. The heat and desire of a few moments ago was slowly draining away, and she was left shivering with cold despair: the bitter, galling knowledge that she had no one else to blame for the situation in which she now found herself. Staring blindly down at her nervously twisting hands, she knew that she had been totally betrayed by her own long-dormant emotions.

'I'm sorry, Stephanie.' Maxim's deep, husky voice seemed to echo around the small room as he continued to stare out of the window. 'What happened just now . . .' He paused, giving a heavy sigh as he brushed a hand roughly through his thick, dark hair.

'Please . . . please go away,' she muttered helplessly.

'No, I'm afraid I can't do that.' He turned around slowly to face her. 'You and I have a lot of things to straighten out between us.'

'But I'm busy . . . the shop . . .' Stephanie hunted desperately in her mind for some way of getting him to leave. She must have a breathing space in which to think what she was going to do.

'No. We're going to talk—here and now,' he said firmly.

Stephanie raised a trembling hand to her head, which was beginning to throb with a dull ache. 'You must see that this isn't either the right time or the right place,' she said, gesturing wearily at her surroundings. 'Certainly not for the sort of discussion you clearly have in mind,' she added bitterly. 'Surely you can wait until I've got home, and . . .'

'Oh, no!' He gave a harsh, sardonic laugh. 'I deliberately chose to come here. I want our discussion to be conducted well away from your home and family.'

'I bet you do! And what about Claire?' she demanded.

He frowned. 'Claire works for me. This has nothing to do with her, and I certainly don't want her involved.'

And neither did she, Stephanie quickly reminded herself, feeling sick and bitterly ashamed at having—even for a fleeting moment —experienced such a sharp, stab of jealousy about her stepdaughter's relationship with Maxim. Oh, lord—what was happening to her?

'Besides which—I know you,' he continued grimly, driving the final nail in her coffin. 'If I gave you half a chance, you'd skip town like you did once before, and I'd have the devil's own job to track you down again. I'm sorry, sweetheart,' he gave a cold, cynical smile, 'but you and I are staying right here.'

'Don't you dare call me that!' she hissed angrily.

He shrugged. 'All this is a complete waste of time. Adam is my son, and . . .' He broke off at the sound of a knock on the door.

'I'm sorry, love,' Lisa said, putting her head around the door. 'You haven't forgotten that I have to go and pick up the children . . . ?'

'Oh, yes, of course.' Stephanie jumped nervously to her feet.

Lisa threw a quick, apologetic grin at Maxim. 'You know how it is with kids—one seems to be forever carting them back and forth to birthday parties, piano lessons, ballet classes—and goodness knows what else!'

'No, I can't say I do know—but I'm looking

forward to finding out,' he drawled smoothly, accompanying his words with a warm, infectious smile.

The damn man uses his charm like a weapon! Stephanie thought grimly as she saw how her normally bright, intelligent assistant was now gazing like a star-struck teenager at the tall American. All he has to do is to flash one of those brilliant megawatt smiles of his, and women fall down around him like ninepins!

'OK, Lisa, I'll be down in a minute,' she told the other woman, who finally managed to break out of her trance-like state, retreating slowly back down the stairs.

'I have to go and see to the shop,' she said, when she was sure they were alone once again. 'We don't close for another half-hour.'

He looked at her for a moment, and then with a quick movement, he scooped up her bag from where she had dropped it on the floor.

'Hey—what do you think you're doing?'

'Does this contain your car keys and purse?' he demanded.

'Yes, but . . .'

Maxim's lips curved into a hateful, mocking grin. 'Then I think I'll hang on to it, since you won't get very far without money or keys, will you?'

'You really are the pits!' she ground out bitterly.

He shrugged. 'Go and see to your shop, Stephanie,' he said slowly, as if speaking to a particularly dim-witted child.

'And what are you going to do while I'm downstairs?' she demanded aggressively. 'I have a lot of important papers in my desk, and there's all the business files and invoices up here as well. I'm not prepared to . . .'

'For heaven's sake!' he swore briefly under his breath. 'I've been away in the States on a very hectic business trip for the past three weeks, and I've come here today straight from the airport.' Maxim raised a hand, running it slowly and wearily across his brow. 'Quite frankly, I'm feeling dead on my feet,' he said heavily. 'So, far from wishing to indulge in industrial espionage —or any other crackpot idea you might have— I'm going to be quite content to just sit up here, and grateful for some peace and quiet.'

She gazed at him with stormy eyes, but there didn't seem to be anything she could do about the situation. Without money, and the keys to both her car and her home, Stephanie knew that she was well and truly stuck. Giving Maxim a scathing glance, which she hoped would convey her loathing and distaste of both him personally, and his ruthless tactics, she stalked across the room, relieving her feelings by slamming the door loudly behind her.

'Hey—where did you find *him*?' Lisa exclaimed as Stephanie entered the shop. 'I've never seen anyone quite so . . . I mean . . . well, I really don't know what to say!'

'That'll be the day,' Stephanie muttered under

her breath.

'Hmm . . . ?'

'Oh, nothing,' she said quickly, realising that her bad temper was all to do with Maxim, and certainly not Lisa's fault.

'But who *is* he? It's funny, though, he does look fairly familiar, although I'm sure I've never seen him before. Have you known him long?'

Stephanie winced, turning quickly away to tidy some sweaters on a shelf. The resemblance between Adam and his father was so striking that she must try and get Maxim away from here as soon as possible. Lisa wasn't the only bright, inquisitive person who would be able to quickly make the connection, especially if she ever saw them both together.

'Well, come on—spill the beans!'

'I met Mr Tyler many years ago in New York, although I haven't seen him for a long time. He . . . er . . . he's just an old friend, that's all,' Stephanie added with a dismissive shrug.

'What do you mean "that's all"?' Lisa's voice rose several octaves. 'Here you are, with one of the most sensationally attractive men I've *ever* seen, and you . . . you just shrug your shoulders!' she added incredulously. 'First Guy Fletcher and now that man upstairs. How can you be so choosy?' she demanded.

'He's a married man,' Stephanie said flatly.

'So, who cares?' Lisa gave a low gurgle of coarse laughter as she put on her coat. 'Frankly, love, he can have the key to my bedroom door *any* night of the week!'

'You really are the end,' Stephanie told her sternly, her lips curving into a reluctant, wry grin despite the fraught, tense confrontation that she knew lay ahead of her.

'Well, love, if you want my advice—which you clearly don't—I'd make up my mind about one or other of the men who seem to be pursuing you,' Lisa said as she opened the door. 'And if that highly charged aura of sexual tension upstairs was anything to go by, I know *just* who I'd put my money on!' she added with a laugh, closing the shop door behind her.

Despite what she'd said to Maxim, Stephanie knew that there was no way she could possibly cope with any customers—not today. Putting up the 'closed' sign on the door, she was just about to turn off the lights when she caught sight of herself in a mirror.

It was all she could do not to shriek out loud with dismay. No wonder Lisa had been looking at her in a most peculiar manner. Her dress looked as if it had been dragged through a hedge backwards, and as for the state of her face and hair . . .

I really, *really* loathe him! she raged silently, flinching at the sight of her tangled and disordered hair. With shaking hands she removed the combs and shook out the long, pale gold locks, before trying to sweep them back up on top of her head again. It didn't look too bad when she'd finished, but she would have given everything she possessed to lay her hands on some make-up. However, it seemed there was nothing she could do to disguise either the hectic flush on her cheeks, or the sight of her lips—still full and swollen from Maxim's kiss.

Hesitating for a moment at the top of the stairs, she took a deep breath as she realised there was no escape. She had no alternative but to face the music and get it over as soon as possible, she told herself grimly, taking a deep breath before slowly opening the door of the apartment.

CHAPTER FOUR

STEPHANIE looked around the room, her blue eyes widening with astonishment. After all her fear and trepidation, she was now amazed to find that the apartment appeared to be completely empty. For a few, brief moments she leaned back against the door, almost overcome with a sense of euphoria and relief, before she forced herself to face the unpalatable truth: unless Maxim had thrown himself out of the window—a fantasy to which she clung for one or two happy seconds— there was no way he could have left without going out through the shop.

The layout of the small apartment was very simple. Bounded by the dimensions of the shop below, it contained a small kitchen near the front door, which itself opened directly into the sitting-room where she was now standing. A doorway led from the sitting-room into a room of the same size, with a bathroom beyond, which she used as a bedroom suite when pressure of business kept her working late at the shop.

With no exit other than the stairs which she had just climbed, it didn't take a very high IQ to know *exactly* where the damn man was, she thought grimly. Walking swiftly across the floor, Stephanie pushed open the door of the

bedroom, to find her worst suspicions confirmed. After having braced herself to face one of the
most critical situations of her life, it came as a
thorough anticlimax to discover that her prota-
gonist was now lying stretched out on the
bed—fast asleep.

She gazed silently down at the lines of tired-
ness and fatigue etched on Maxim's tanned face.
He looked exhausted, and she was surprised to
find herself suddenly feeling concerned and
worried about him for a moment, before quickly
pulling herself together. It would be absolutely
fatal to make the mistake of forgetting the
danger he posed—both to her family and her
present safe, secure way of life.

Noticing that Maxim had removed his shoes,
and that the jacket of his dark grey suit together
with his navy blue and red silk tie were lying on
a small chair by the bed, she walked quietly
across the room and opened the lid of an old oak
chest. There wasn't much heating in the
apartment and, as much as she disliked the man,
she really couldn't allow him to catch cold,
Stephanie told herself as she carefully covered
the long length of his lean figure with a soft,
fleecy blanket.

He had told her he always suffered from jet
lag, she recalled. Moving quietly across the room
to sit down in an armchair, she remembered how
it had seemed so ridiculous that a dynamic, high-
powered businessman should be pole-axed by
such a trivial complaint.

Stephanie sighed as she tried to keep the mists

of memory at bay, but it was difficult when the man who had once meant more to her than life itself was lying only six feet or so away.

She had been so ecstatically happy, during those few summer days ten years ago. Maybe it was the contrast between that overwhelmingly joyous time when she had been almost walking on air, and the grief and desolation of Maxim's desertion, which had left her in such a state of wretched torment?

Stephanie shivered as she recalled the fearful, harrowing feelings of desperation and panic which had swept over her at the discovery, only a few weeks after he'd gone, that she was expecting Maxim's baby. If only she hadn't been so young; if there had been any close relatives or friends who would have either helped her themselves, or directed her to those who could—she might not have taken the action she did.

Not that she had ever really intended to jump off that bridge into the cold, murky depths of the Hudson River, but at the time she had been so desperately unhappy, and half out of her mind with pain and misery, that she hadn't known what she was doing. It wasn't until someone had taken a firm hold of her arm, and the clipped tones of a strange English accent had spoken softly in her ear before leading her safely back to his car parked by the wharf, that she'd begun to realise how foolish she had been.

'However unhappy you may be—ending your life isn't the answer,' the man had said, after he'd taken her to a small family restaurant, ignoring her protests as he insisted that she had a good hot meal. 'I know what I'm talking about,' his voice had sounded bleak and desolate. 'Because I've been in exactly the same situation myself.'

During the next couple of hours, Stephanie had been surprised to find herself telling the man, James Hammond, all about the desperate position in which she found herself. Maybe it was because he was a complete stranger, but it had been a tremendous relief to unburden herself of her problems. To explain that, having left the mid-West to come to art school in New York, she now had only a few friends, all of whom had left town for the summer vacation.

'Isn't there anyone you can turn to?' he had asked, frowning with concern when she had dolefully shaken her head. 'Are you quite sure you want to keep the baby?'

'Oh, yes!' she had gasped, clasping her thin arms about her trembling body. 'I could never . . . I mean, it's all I've got left of M-Maxim,' she'd added, trying to blink back the tears in her eyes. 'What's worrying me so much is that I just don't know how I'm going to be able to support the two of us after the baby is born.'

Over the course of the meal they discovered that they had many interests in common: they liked the same books and films, and they were both crazy about music and opera. She had also learned that James was an accountant. He had apparently flown over to New York for a business conference, and was due to return to England in a few days' time. He also told her that he, too, was desperately unhappy at the recent death of his much-loved wife, and that he had two young children, aged eleven and thirteen.

By the time he had driven her back to her apartment—leaving her with the telephone number of his hotel and a strict injunction that she was to call him if she was ever feeling desperate again—Stephanie had felt more at peace with herself. Although James was a complete stranger, he had offered her kindness and comfort, for which she was very grateful.

Since he was soon going back to England, she hadn't ever expected to see James Hammond again, and she was surprised when he called at her apartment two days later. But not half so surprised as she was after listening to what he had to say.

'You want me to go with you to England? To be your housekeeper?' she'd queried, gazing at him in astonishment.

'No . . . er . . . not quite.' James' cheeks had reddened. 'As I believe I told you—I was very much in love with my wife. We were everything to each other, and I know that I'll never fall in love again,' he added, his face etched with pain. 'The firm of accountants I work for are very understanding about giving me time off, but . . .' He had shrugged his shoulders and sighed deeply. 'Richard and Claire need more than a part-time father, and the various housekeepers I've engaged have not been a success.'

Stephanie had frowned. 'Yes, but I don't quite see . . .'

'I want you to marry me—in name only, of course,' he'd added quickly, his cheeks flushing again. 'My children need a kind, warm and loving stepmother, and someone who would also create a happy home atmosphere. Although we hardly know each other, I'm quite sure that you would be all of those things.' He turned to look around the apartment which, though very small, had been made bright and comfortable with home-made soft furnishings, the walls decorated with her paintings.

'In return,' he continued as she gazed at him with stunned eyes, 'I would look after you and the baby. And since we would be married when your child is born, he or she would be quite legitimate. I know that in this day and age, being born out of wedlock is not supposed to matter,' he'd added with a rueful smile. 'But I don't think the children involved would necessarily agree.'

'I really can't . . .'

'Please at least think about it,' James had urged. 'We both have problems—and my suggestion of a contract between us might well solve them. I'll come back for your answer tomorrow.'

Stephanie had spent a sleepless night, tossing and turning as she considered the 'contract'

James had proposed for their mutual benefit. In the end, of course, it was the future welfare of the baby she was carrying which had finally tipped the balance, and which had led her to agree to his proposition.

After putting her apartment in the hands of a real estate broker, she had flown back to England with James. Her only stipulation had been that she should meet his children before finally agreeing to marry him, but Richard and Claire had been cautiously welcoming, and when their new baby brother had arrived both of them had been delighted.

It hadn't been easy adapting to a completely strange life in England, but James had been a tower of strength—especially towards the end of her pregnancy and during the birth of Adam—and it was at his insistence that no one, not even his own children, should know that he wasn't the baby's father.

'I want your son to grow up in a atmosphere of love and security. Therefore, as far as I'm concerned, he's *our* child,' James had said firmly. 'You've created a wonderful home for both myself and my children, and if we're all so much happier than we've been for a very long time, it's entirely due to you,' he'd added with a warm smile. 'In fact, as far as I can see, there's nothing to stop us all living happily ever after!'

And so they had, until James—who'd never had a day's illness in his life—had so unexpectedly collapsed in his office one day, and had died of a heart attack a few minutes later.

At the memory of that intensely unhappy time, Stephanie rose quickly to her feet, going over to the window and staring blindly down at the empty arcade below. Despite all that had happened to her, she'd managed to keep a roof over the children's heads, and to provide the necessities of life for them all. It had been a hard, upward slog to start with, but she was now becoming very successful in her business, and with the two older children grown up, and only Adam to look after, her life had become so much easier. Surely, if there was any justice in the world, she ought now to be free of the man who had caused her so much heartache and torment all those years ago?

She turned to look back at the sleeping figure on the bed and saw that he was now awake, his green eyes beneath their heavy lids regarding her with a firm, steady determination that chilled her blood.

'Thank you for not letting me freeze to death,' he said, throwing aside the blanket. 'I still haven't got used to British central heating—or rather, the lack of it,' he added with a wry grimace.

Stephanie shrugged. 'There is nothing so cold and draughty as an old English mansion. So, it sounds as though you're going to be in for a thoroughly uncomfortable time in your new house, doesn't it?' she said, with a marked absence of sympathy in her voice.

'You're all heart!' he murmured, giving her such a warm, infectious grin that her heart almost missed a beat for a moment, before his next words rapidly brought her crashing back down to earth. 'As far as Adam is concerned, I hope that now you've had time for reflection you'll stop trying to deny the undeniable,' he said, swinging his legs down on to the floor and brushing his hands through his thick, black hair.

'I don't have to confirm or deny anything,' she retorted, trying to keep calm. 'My son's birth certificate states—very clearly—that he is the child of myself and my late husband, James Hammond. And quite frankly, Maxim, if you think that you can suddenly invade my life with some specious claim to be Adam's father, then you are very much mistaken!'

'No, it is you who are mistaken—or rather, maybe you should have kept more up to date with medical science,' he said dryly, bending down to do up his shoes. 'Haven't you heard about genetic fingerprinting?'

'What on earth are you talking about?'

'It is only one of the many aids of identification in use nowadays. Believe me, Stephanie,' he drawled, not bothering to hide the threat in his voice, 'it merely needs a small blood sample from both Adam and myself to confirm—*beyond all shadow of legal doubt*—that he is indisputably my son!'

She stared at him for a moment. 'I—I don't believe you,' she muttered, desperately trying to recall what little she knew about genes and the classification of blood groups.

'Whether you believe me or not is immaterial,' he said brutally, standing up and walking through into the small bathroom to wash his hands and face. 'The plain fact is that I'm Adam's father, and——Can I have a towel?' he called out, raising his voice above the sound of the water running from the taps.

'What? Oh . . . yes, just a minute.' Her lips tightened with anger. Here they were, in the midst of one of the most important discussions of her life, and she was stupid enough to be acting like some dutiful handmaiden. *Maybe I should just tie it very tightly around his neck*, she thought viciously as she removed the small towel from a cupboard. And what was she doing, meekly letting him walk all over her like this? It was time she started fighting back—and to hell with the finer points of the Queensberry Rules!

'Here you are,' she said, going into the bathroom and handing him the towel.

'Thank you. As I was saying . . .'

'I've been listening to what *you* have been saying all afternoon,' she snapped. 'But now it's my turn to point out one or two things about which you've been strangely silent. For instance, you appear to have absolutely no compunction about destroying all my family relationships, but we haven't heard a word about your wife, have we? How is she going to feel when she hears this wild story about you having fathered my son? After all,' she added, not bothering to hide the scorn and derision in her voice, 'it's not *exactly* guaranteed to increase your state of happily married bliss, is it?'

His tall figure froze for a moment, the lines deepening in his face as he stared blindly at his reflection in the small mirror over the handbasin.

'Well, well!' She gave a shrill, triumphant laugh. 'It looks as though clever Mr Tyler hasn't thought of *that* little problem!'

Maxim gave a heavy sigh, and slowly turned around to face her. 'My wife is dead,' he said bleakly.

'Oh, hell—I'm sorry. I wouldn't have said . . . I mean, if I'd known, I'd never . . .'

'Estelle died four years ago,' he continued, ignoring her breathless apology. 'So there is nothing either of us can do to hurt her now.'

She gasped, the rasping agony in his voice hitting her like a fierce blow, her eyes wide with shock as his words echoed around the small tiled room.

His mouth was twisted with pain as he ran his hand wearily through his thick black hair. 'It was a good try, Stephanie,' he said harshly, his eyes hard as stones, sweeping contemptuously over her trembling figure. 'But I'm afraid you're going to find that 'clever Mr Tyler' has you over a barrel. And the sooner you realise it, the better.'

Stephanie stared at him with dazed eyes. Although she heard what he was saying, the

grim implication of his words was lost beneath a
blinding flash of revelation which left her feeling
completely devastated.

*What a complete and utter imbecile she'd been all
these years!* The revelation of her incredible folly
cut through her heart like a knife of cold steel. It
was his *wife* that Maxim had loved all the time,
not her at all. And, as the significance of that
discovery slowly filled her tired mind, the tiny
flame that she had held so secretly in her heart
for the past ten years now flickered and died.
She only had to look at the tortured expression
on his face to know the truth: she had never
meant anything to him—nothing at all.

Almost gasping with agony, she turned
quickly away. 'I—I must go, I . . .'

'Oh, no, you don't!' Maxim growled, his hand
quickly grasping her arm, and swinging her
around to face him with such force that she
found herself clasped to his firm chest. Shocked
by his abrupt action, she shivered as she gazed
into his hard green eyes.

'Please let me go,' she begged.

'No.'

She trembled at the flat note of determination
in his voice. 'We . . . we can't stay here all night.
I must have time . . . time to think . . .' she told
him breathlessly, trying to wriggle free of his
iron grip.

'I'm not letting you out of my sight. Not until
we've finished our discussion,' he drawled
silkily, looking down at her flushed cheeks, the

blue eyes wide with distress, and her quivering full lips.

Pressed so tightly against his body, her legs began to shake as she felt the warmth of his chest through the thin silk shirt, open at the neck to display the strong column of his tanned throat. The hard, ruthless expression on the face so close to her own was gradually softening, the glinting topaz lights in his green eyes playing havoc with her senses, causing her to feel faint and dizzy as she stared mesmerised at his wide, sensual mouth.

It was suddenly all too much for her to cope with. 'I—I simply can't face any more!' she cried, as she wrenched herself away from his iron grip, and stumbled blindly into the bedroom, her eyes filled with tears.

'Stephanie, I . . .'

'For heaven's sake, don't you understand? Can't you see what you're doing to m-me?' she sobbed, whirling around to face him as he followed her into the room. 'You're d-destroying my whole life!'

'That's ridiculous,' he told her sternly, a muscle beating in his clenched jaw.

'No—it's not!' she stormed, heedless of the hot tears running down her pale cheeks. 'You haven't given a thought to how all this is going to affect Adam, have you? How do you think he's going to feel, when a man he's barely met suddenly announces that he's his father? But why should you care, just as long as you can establish your so-called "rights"?' she raged.

Maxim's cheeks were flushed beneath his tanned skin, and he looked distinctly uncomfortable. 'You're talking complete nonsense,' he grated. 'For goodness' sake, be quiet! Calm down.'

'No—I damned well won't!' she yelled back at him, not caring what she said as the emotional stress and strain of the last few weeks rose to the surface, and she lost all control in the overwhelming desire to hit back at the man who had caused her such pain, shaking her head so fiercely that the combs fell away, allowing the wild cloud of pale gold hair to swirl unrestrained about her shoulders.

'I don't care if the whole world and his wife can hear me—thanks to you, they're soon going to know all about my "wicked past" anyway, right? So what does a bit of gossip matter when you're going to destroy my relationship with my stepdaughter, and . . . and take my child away from me . . .?' she wailed, throwing herself down on to the bed in a wild storm of tears.

She was dimly aware of Maxim swearing violently under his breath, before he came and sat down on the bed beside her, gathering her limp, weeping figure into his arms.

'Oh, Stephanie . . . don't cry like this, you'll make yourself ill,' he murmured, continuing to hold her in his firm embrace until her storm of tears diminished.

'I—I'm s-sorry . . .' she muttered helplessly,

deep sobs continuing to rack her slim frame. 'I d-don't know what's come over me. I'm truly not the sort of woman who . . .'

'Hush, now. I promise you there's no need for these tears,' he assured her, raising his hand to softly brush the damp tendrils of hair from her brow.

The heat of his body, pressed so closely to her own trembling figure, was playing havoc with her fast dwindling reserves of emotional stability. For one mad, completely insane moment, she weakly allowed herself to lean against his broad shoulder, mindlessly savouring the strength of his arms and the warmth of his fingers as they moved down over her flushed cheeks, drawing back the curtain of hair from one side of her face. But his gentle touch brought back so many bitter-sweet memories, clutching at her heart and filling her with such pain, that it was all she could do not to begin weeping again.

'Come on, sweetheart—that's quite enough,' Maxim said firmly, taking out a large white handkerchief to gently wipe the fresh droplets of tears from her wet, spiky eyelashes.

'Now, Stephanie,' he added, 'I know that it may have come as something of a shock—our meeting each other again, here in England. But why in heaven's name should you think that I wish to take Adam away from you, hmm?'

'Because . . . because you've been so . . . so awful—so threatening!' She seized the handkerchief and fiercely blew her nose. 'And you s-said . . .'

'I certainly never said that I would try and remove your child from your care,' he declared. 'What sort of man do you think I am, for pete's sake?'

She gasped, giving a slightly hysterical laugh and impatiently brushing aside her long cloud of hair as she stared up into the face only inches away from her own.

'I don't have to think—I *know* just what a ruthless b-bastard you are!' she grated savagely, her body still shaken by occasional hiccups. 'You don't care what you do, or who you hurt.'

'That's simply not true!'

'Oh, no?' She gave a shaky, bitter laugh. 'After the way you walked out on me in New York, I know better, don't I?'

He sighed heavily. 'There are so many things we have yet to discuss. Our past relationship, and . . .'

'That's history,' she interrupted him quickly. 'It was dead and buried well over ten years ago. My only interest now is Adam—and I swear I'll kill you before I let you get your hands on him!'

He frowned and shook his head impatiently. 'For heaven's sake, Stephanie—stop talking nonsense!' He paused. 'Look, I'm willing to admit that I well may have been unkind just now . . . and possibly more insensitive than I realised.'

'That's putting it mildly!'

'All right—but can you please try and see

things from my side of the fence? I realise that you may have been surprised by my sudden reappearance in your life—but have you *any* idea of how I felt when I first saw Adam? It was like being hit on the head by a ton weight.' He gave a wry, crooked smile. 'I don't think I've ever been so shocked and stunned by anything in the whole of my life as I was when I realised that I had a child—*a son!*'

'He's not . . . Adam is nothing to do with you,' she protested, determined to protect her child, despite knowing in her heart that it was hopeless to keep denying the truth.

Maxim frowned. 'OK, let's get this business sorted out once and for all,' he said firmly, lifting her up in his arms and settling her back against the pillows by the bedhead. 'Now, Stephanie, there are some basic facts which you really must accept,' he said quietly, sitting down beside her and taking her hands in his. 'It's important you realise that right from the very first moment I laid eyes on him there has never been the shadow of a doubt in my mind about Adam's paternity. So, whether you confirm or deny the fact that I'm his father, it's immaterial as far as I'm concerned, because I *know*—with every fibre of my being—that he's my son.'

She tried to give a casual shrug, determined not to admit how his words had shaken her. Surely he couldn't be that certain? Or was it really possible for a blood tie to be so strong that it transcended all normal forms of recognition?

'Secondly, there's no doubt that Adam and I bear a close resemblance to each other,' he continued. 'So, whatever happens—even if you continue to deny that he's my son—other people are going to draw their own obvious conclusions.'

'Only if we're living in the same village,' she said quickly. 'It isn't too late for either you or me to go away and . . .'

'Oh, come on!' Maxim drawled, raising a sardonic dark eyebrow. 'Don't you think it's about time you started using your brain? Not only is it totally impractical for you to give up your home and your business, but I've just spent a few million dollars buying the Stow-under-Hill estate. So the suggestion that one of us should take off for foreign parts is clearly ridiculous!'

'But what are we going to do?' she exclaimed helplessly, feeling as if she was going to burst into tears again at any minute.

'Ah—I'm glad you said "we". At least you're getting around to admitting that I do have a right to be involved in this matter,' he said with a wry smile.

'I don't see how that makes the whole rotten business any better,' she muttered, staring down at her hands, which were still tightly clasped within his long, tanned fingers.

'Providing we can agree and co-operate together, there is absolutely no need for all this doom and gloom,' he said firmly. 'I have been stressing my moral and legal right of access to my son solely to impress upon you that I'm deadly serious. You have denied me access or any knowledge of Adam for the past nine years,' Maxim's voice hardened, 'and while there may have been good reasons for your doing so—the situation has now changed. I intend to be fully involved in the remaining years of my son's upbringing, and it's perfectly natural I should wish to do so. However,' he added, 'I have *no* intention of creating any unnecessary problems for either you or Adam.'

'It won't work. The whole situation is imposs-ible!' Stephanie cried, wrenching her hands away and quickly grabbing his handkerchief once again.

'No, it's not,' he said firmly. 'Although, of course, I want to see as much of my son as I can, I'm well aware that the situation has to be handled with kid gloves. Hopefully, over a period of time, he can come to understand that I'm his father, without it being too much of a shock. Goodness knows—he seems bright enough!' Maxim gave a short bark of rueful laughter. 'And from the purely financial angle, you must see that there is so much I can do for him.'

She glared at him over the top of the white cotton handkerchief, her blue eyes flashing with anger.

'No,' he said curtly, accurately reading her mind as she opened her mouth to protest. 'Of course I'm not stupid enough to imagine that I can buy the boy's affection. However, as my son and heir, Adam would obviously have many more advantages and opportunities in life than he has at present. Why not think about it for a minute, hmm?' he added, rising to his feet and going over to the chair where he had left his tie and jacket.

Viewing his tall figure as he put on his tie and shrugged his broad shoulders into the jacket, Stephanie realised that she couldn't ignore his last words. From the discreet gleam of his gold Rolex watch to the immaculate tailoring of his handmade suit, Maxim personified a standard of wealth and affluence that was way beyond anything that she could provide for her son.

It didn't matter at the moment, of course. Although he was intellectually very clever, in many ways Adam was still a typical boy, and far more interested in his bicycle and various hobbies than in future riches. But what about the future? How would he react when he was older? Would he hold it against her if, by any action on her part, she had kept him from his rightful inheritance?

'You look exhausted.'

Stephanie gazed wearily up at Maxim. He was right. She was feeling so tired and emotionally drained by the events of the afternoon that she couldn't seem to think clearly. She could outline all the problems in her mind, but any solution— or even a partial answer—seemed completely beyond her.

'Come on—I'm taking you home.'

'What?'

'There's no need to look so surprised,' he drawled mockingly. 'For the past two hours you've been telling me that you wanted to leave this apartment. Or have you changed your mind?'

'No, but . . .'

He gave an impatient sigh. 'I'm cold, you're tired, and I imagine that we could both do with a good, hot meal. Besides, no woman looks good when she's been crying—and you look terrible,' he added brutally.

'Well, if I am—it's all your fault!' she retorted bitterly, all further protest forgotten as she quickly slipped off the bed and hurried into the bathroom.

'Terrible' was a totally inadequate word, she thought grimly, staring horrified at the sight of her blotchy, tear-stained face.

There wasn't much she could do—not while the beastly man was so obviously, and impatiently, tapping his foot outside the bathroom door. Not that she really cared what she looked like, of course. She just wanted to get home. Stephanie couldn't remember ever feeling such a fierce longing for the sanctuary of the Old Barn. At least in her own house she could be assured of peace and quiet, and a safe, if temporary, haven from Maxim's dominant personality. However, after quickly brushing her hair into some sort of order, and following the swift application of lipstick and powder, she did manage to feel slightly more presentable by the time he escorted her from the apartment.

The heavy silence in the back of the luxurious limousine was almost deafening—if that wasn't a contradiction in terms, Stephanie thought glumly, staring out of the window at the darkness beyond.

'I don't care what you say, I still think that this is a stupid arrangement,' she muttered, turning to glare at the man sitting next to her in the back of the large Rolls-Royce. 'I feel a perfect fool riding around in this huge limousine. What's happened to that glamorous Ferrari of yours—crashed it already, have you?' she enquired nastily.

'Of course not!' he snapped, and then clicked his teeth with annoyance at having been prodded into responding to Stephanie's barbed comment. 'As I told you—I've just flown in from the States. And, knowing that I would be tired from the flight, I ordered my chauffeur to meet me at the airport and drive me straight up here,' he added in a calmer voice.

'Well, you're not "ordering" me around! I'm perfectly capable of driving myself.'

'Why don't you just shut up, Stephanie?' Maxim drawled caustically.

She winced as the hard, underlying tone of his voice washed over her like a douche of icy cold water. It was only her refusal to admit that she

was practically down and out for the count that
gave her the strength to continue to defy him.

'But I'm going to need my own car to get to
work tomorrow. Besides which . . .' She quickly
broke off to add, '*Hey*! You've taken a wrong
turning. This isn't the way to my house.'

She and Maxim had already had a stand-up
row in the car park behind her shop. It was only
the presence of the uniformed chauffeur—
addressed by Maxim as 'Jenkins', and who had
obviously been patiently waiting for his
employer for the past few hours—which had
prevented her from really letting rip. As it was,
she hadn't had any choice but to accept a lift,
Maxim having flatly refused to allow her to drive
herself home, on the ridiculous grounds that she
was too upset. She'd been arguing about his
high-handed arrangements all the way back to
Stow-under-Hill, and now the loathsome man
seemed to have forgotten where she lived.

'You should have told the chauffeur to have
taken that road to the left,' she grumbled. 'He's
going to have to turn around by the Cross Keys.'

'No, I don't think so.'

She snorted with derision. 'I've had a house in
this village for the last seven years, and however
"upset" you might think I am, I do still happen
to know where I live!'

'Of course you do,' he murmured blandly.
'But we're being driven to *my* home . . .'

'*What?*'

'. . . to have dinner and continue our discussion in more salubrious surroundings. I know you'll be interested to see the alterations I've made to the manor house,' he added smoothly.

'No, I damn well won't!' she snapped, her anger fuelled by the clear note of amusement in his voice. 'Take me home—at once!'

But his only reply was a maddening rumble of sardonic laughter.

Trembling with rage, she glowered at Maxim's shadowy profile in the dim light of the street lamps. Goodness knows, she had always abhorred violence of any kind. But if there was anything she could do—right this minute—to wipe the hateful man off the face of the earth, she wouldn't have the slightest hesitation in doing so.

CHAPTER FIVE

'WOULD you care for some more trifle?'

'Oh, goodness me—no! It—er—it was really delicious,' Stephanie added hurriedly. 'But I couldn't possibly manage to eat any more.'

And that is certainly *no* exaggeration, she told herself as Maxim pressed a bell to summon his housekeeper. After lunch in the restaurant with Guy, and staggering through this rich, three-course dinner here at the manor house, it wasn't surprising that she was now feeling distinctly queasy. All that wine hadn't helped, either!

Stephanie tried to calculate just how many glasses of alcohol she'd consumed. Quite apart from the large gin and tonic on first entering the house, there had been a dry sherry with the almond and watercress soup; white burgundy with the turbot kebabs in a pink shrimp sauce; and a Château d'Yquem, just now, with the orange caramel trifle. Wow! At this rate she was going to float out of the house—always providing, of course, that she could persuade Maxim to let her go.

Gazing fixedly down at the polished mahogany surface of the table as the house-keeper, Mrs Jenkins, came into the dining-room to remove their plates, Stephanie wondered just how soon she could hope to escape from his clutches. Casting a quick sideways glance through her lashes at the hard, determined features of the man sitting at the end of the table, she didn't feel that she had any grounds for optimism.

She must remember that Maxim was capable of just about anything, Stephanie warned herself grimly. And the more devious, underhand and downright tricky the scheme—the better he was sure to like it! On the other hand . . . well, despite her worst fears, she had to admit that right from the moment they'd arrived here tonight he had been playing the part of a very polite and thoroughly considerate host. It was a good act—although it didn't fool her, of course. However, under the benign influence of delicious food and wine, she had found her raw, savage anger at having being virtually kidnapped gradually slipping away. And since he'd confined their conversation to innocuous subjects, such as the restoration and interior decoration of the old Jacobean manor house, they had managed to get through the meal without any major disagreements. Unfortunately, knowing Maxim's hard, tough personality, it clearly wasn't a situation that was likely to continue.

He waited until the housekeeper had left the room and then leaned back in his chair, the jacket of his suit open to reveal the strong, muscular contours of his chest.

'Would you like some cheese? Or maybe some fruit?' he added when she shook her head.

'No—nothing more, thank you,' she muttered.

'Then shall we go and have our coffee in the study?'

Feeling like a lamb being led to the slaughter, she sighed and rose reluctantly to her feet.

'I know you'd prefer to stay safely in the dining-room,' he murmured sardonically, taking her arm and ignoring the stiff rigidity of her figure as they crossed the large, marble-floored hall. 'But I don't like to keep Mrs Jenkins working too late. She and her husband are still in the process of unpacking their belongings—and with the builders still doing up their apartment in the east wing, it's all a bit chaotic for them,' he added, as he opened a door and stood aside for her to enter the room.

Tilly had been quite right, she thought, looking about the room. It wasn't as grand or as spacious as the huge drawing-room, into which she had been ushered on first entering Maxim's house. But it was obvious that here, too, no expense had been spared.

Although a large, red-leather-topped desk was set in front of the bow window, framed by heavy curtains in a rich crimson brocade, it was the only functional piece of furniture that would justify calling the room a study. Possibly 'library' would be a better word, since richly bound books lined the walls either side of the large fireplace, blending with the dark oak panelling to create an atmosphere of calm, peaceful elegance.

Gazing at the deep colours of the silky Persian carpet covering the floor, and the decorative eighteenth-century Chelsea porcelain figures on the oak mantelpiece, Stephanie almost sighed out loud with envy. Like the immaculately cooked and served meal they'd just had, amid all that shining crystal and silver in the dining-room, it all smacked of a great deal of money; but money which had been put to the very best possible use. And, stifling an unworthy impulse which had originally led her to hope that Maxim's taste would prove to be truly awful, she now had to admit that his home was one of the most charming and beautifully decorated houses she had ever seen.

'Why don't you sit down, and make yourself comfortable, hmm?'

Said the spider to the fly? she asked herself, viewing with considerable apprehension the back of Maxim's tall figure as he walked across the room. However, after hesitating for a moment, she sank down into one of the large, heavily cushioned sofas ranged on either side of the roaring log fire.

'You seem to have quite a lot of books in here,' she murmured, gazing up at the row upon row of leather-bound volumes. 'Have you got around to actually reading any of them yet?'

He gave no sign of having noticed the caustic note in her voice. 'Yes, I've read most of them—

one way or another. I collect first editions, mainly of Trollope and Dickens,' he explained quietly. 'Although the bulk of the collection is still at my home in the States, of course,' he added, opening an oak panel to reveal shelves containing glasses and some heavy, crystal decanters.

Stephanie could feel a deep flush spreading over her pale cheeks as she realised that she had just succeeded in making a fool of herself. And serve you right—that's what you get for trying to be too clever, she told herself bleakly, leaning forward to pour a cup of black coffee from a tray on the table in front of her. She ought to have known—and who better?—that it was a total waste of time to try and score points off Maxim.

'A brandy?' he asked, turning as he poured a drink for himself.

'No, thank you,' she said quickly.

'I think you should,' he said, walking back across the room. 'Besides, it will help you to relax,' he added firmly, ignoring the shake of her head as he put a glass down on the table beside her.

Stephanie gazed nervously down at the jet-black liquid in her small coffee-cup as he joined her on the sofa. Help her to relax? That was a laugh! Why else did he think she had been tossing back all that wine at dinner? It certainly hadn't been because she was an incipient alcoholic. In fact, her only object had been to try and anaesthetise her nerves, which had been at

screaming pitch by the time she'd been marched
into this house. And she had succeeded—to a
certain extent. Unfortunately, it was beginning
to look as if she'd also managed, at one and the
same time, to deaden all her sense of caution and
prudence. Why else should she be sitting here,
only inches away from Maxim's tall, rangy
figure, when if she had an ounce of self-
preservation left in her veins she ought by now
to be on her feet and sprinting through that door
as fast as her legs could carry her?

'Cheers.'

'Hmm . . .?'

'I think we should drink to our future relationship,' he drawled, raising his glass. 'Why don't
you join me?'

'Because I'm not going to join in that toast,
and I have *no* intention of drinking any more
alcohol,' she retorted.

He gave a snort of wry amusement. 'Well, I
guess that's what you'd call being blunt and to
the point!'

She shrugged, and then concentrated on pouring herself another cup of liquid caffeine, before
trying to get back to the safe, harmless type of
conversation they had been having at the dinner-
table.

'This is a lovely room,' she said, turning to
look about her. 'How long will it be before the
builders finish doing up the rest of the house?
You must have had hordes of people working
night and day to have got so much done in such

a short time.'

Maxim gave a low laugh. 'Oh, come on, Stephanie! We have already discussed my purchase of this house *ad nauseum*, and I am heartily bored with the subject.' He tipped the remaining brandy down his throat and placed the empty glass on the table in front of them. 'It's now time we talked about more intimate family matters.'

'I was afraid you were going to say that,' she muttered, the china cup rattling on its saucer as she tried to control her nervous, trembling hands. 'And if you're going to start threatening me about Adam again . . .'

'No—that's not my intention,' he said firmly. 'Although, naturally, I do want to know more about my son. For instance, he obviously isn't at home with you at the moment, so I imagine you've placed him in an English boarding-school?'

'Yes, I . . .' She hesitated, and then took a deep breath as she realised that, whether she liked it or not, Maxim did have a moral right to ask questions about his son.

'Adam has been at a local boarding-school for about a year,' she said. 'He . . . I'm told he's a very clever child . . .'

Maxim smiled. 'Yes, I rather gathered that he must be—he was certainly quite correct about the mess I'd made of my chess game!' he added ruefully.

'Yes, well . . . Adam does seem to be very happy at his school, and most of his weekends are free, but I obviously would prefer to have him living at home all the time. In fact, if you want to know the honest truth, I still feel a bit guilty about sending him away so young. However, when James died and left us with hardly anything—except for that large house in Islington—I truly didn't have much of a choice,' she assured him earnestly.

'Relax, Stephanie. No one's blaming you for any decision you may have taken in those circumstances,' he said quietly, leaning over to remove the coffee-cup from her hands.

'The hard facts of life were that I had to either go out to work, or start up a business,' she continued. 'That meant selling our home in London, and moving to live in the country, where housing in so much cheaper. And once the shop and my knitting business got going . . .' She shrugged. 'The whole thing has snowballed to such an extent, and I'm now so busy all the time, that sending Adam away to school seemed to be the best solution.'

'What made you decide to move to this area of the Cotswolds?' he asked.

'Well, I managed to get quite a lot of money for the house in London—enough to lease a shop in Broadway and to buy an old, decrepit barn here in Stow-under-Hill. As to why I chose this part of the country . . .' She gave a slight laugh. 'You'll think I'm crazy if I tell you the real reason.'

He raised a dark eyebrow. 'And that was . . .?'

'It was the name of the village,' she grinned. 'Maybe I was kind of homesick—or whatever. But as soon as I saw the advertisement for a shop to let in a village I'd never heard of, called *Broadway*—well . . . I'm not sure how to describe it, except that it seemed as though it was some sort of omen.' She shrugged her shoulders and gave him a wry smile. 'Anyway, I just knew it was going to be the right place for me. A reminder of my time in New York, and . . .' Her voice died away, her cheeks reddening beneath his steady gaze. Oh, lord! Why hadn't she kept her stupid mouth shut?

Maxim, too, clearly felt the reference to New York had been an unfortunate one. She watched apprehensively as his mouth tightened into a hard line, and he rose abruptly from the sofa, going over to the decanter to refill his glass.

'I can't forgive myself . . .' He sighed heavily, turning around to face her. 'You should have told me that you were expecting my child.' His voice was harsh and accusatory.

'How could I? By the time I discovered I was pregnant, you'd said 'goodbye' and gone back to your wife,' Stephanie retorted bleakly.

'Nevertheless, we could have worked something out,' he told her fiercely.

'Like what?' she groaned impatiently. 'Or are you going to try and suggest that your wife would have been ecstatically happy, and thrilled to bits to hear about the happy event?' she added with heavy sarcasm.

Maxim swore violently under his breath. 'I'm not denying that there would have been problems,' he ground out as he began to pace up and down over the silk carpet. 'But have you never thought about *my* feelings in this matter?'

Stephanie gazed at him with blank astonishment for a moment, scarcely able to believe her ears. 'Now I've heard it all!' she gasped, before giving a high-pitched, hysterical laugh. 'Believe me, *your* tender feelings were the very *last* thing I was ever likely to think about!'

'Well, why don't you try thinking about them now?' he demanded roughly. 'Just how do you think I feel, knowing that you've been forced into poverty—and had to go out to work—in order to support my son?'

'Hang on!' she snapped. 'I and my family were never *that* poor. And although I did need to work—what's wrong with that, I'd like to know? Besides, only a fool would make the mistake of thinking that money equals happiness,' she added scathingly.

'Thank you—but I don't need a lecture on moral philosophy!' he growled, thrusting a furiously impatient hand through his dark hair. 'All it needed was one word from you, telling me that you were expecting my child—*just one word*!' he thundered. 'You must know that I would have made sure you and Adam were properly looked after.'

The raw bitterness in his voice echoed harshly around the room, and Stephanie shut her eyes for a moment, leaning wearily back against the sofa cushions.

'What's the point of all this?' she said at last in a thin, tired voice. 'Mentally whipping yourself or shouting at me isn't going to achieve anything, is it?'

Maxim paused in his restless pacing for a moment, throwing her a searching, steely glance from beneath his heavy lids. 'You'd better drink up that brandy—you look as though you need it.'

'No, I . . .' She sighed and shook her head, her eyes following the movements of his tall figure as he continued to stride back and forth across the carpet with the lithe and supple grace of a menacing, predatory animal.

The cut of his dark suit was clearly designed to emphasise the strong, lean body beneath the clothes—the broad shoulders, deep chest and slim waist of a superbly fit man. His black hair, glinting like a raven's wings beneath the light from the chandeliers, swept down over his well-shaped head to touch the edge of his collar. Watching as he brushed a hand through its thick fullness, Stephanie felt an iron band of fear suddenly clutching at her heart.

She'd been trying to fight it all evening, but she couldn't fool herself any longer. It wasn't all that sound and fury just now which was so frightening, or the ever-present danger he posed to her way of life which was uppermost in her mind. She was appalled to find that, despite the long gap of ten years, Maxim still possessed an alarmingly dangerous sexual attraction for her, and it was one she was finding impossible to ignore.

Almost as though he had read her thoughts, Maxim ceased to pace the carpet, his eyes narrowing as he stared down at her flushed cheeks. Swiftly turning her face away from his searching gaze, she trembled as he walked over and sat down beside her once more.

'I'm sorry,' he said with a heavy sigh. 'You're quite right. There's nothing to be gained by raking over the past. It's the future we must think about now, hmm?'

She nodded silently, not trusting her voice as he picked up the glass of brandy from beside her empty coffee-cup, placing it firmly in her hands. 'You're looking a bit pale—this ought to make you feel better.'

'No, I really don't think . . .'

'Drink it!' he commanded tersely.

Stephanie sighed helplessly, and then with a reckless gesture that she knew she was going to regret she tipped the fiery stream of liquid down her throat.

'When I said ''drink'', I didn't mean ''gulp''!' Maxim said drily, leaning closer to pat her back as she choked and spluttered, gasping for breath.

'Good lord!' she croaked hoarsely as the heat ran wildly through her body. 'What on earth was that—fire water?'

'Kindly don't insult the best Napoleon brandy,' he grinned. 'Relax, sweetheart. You'll feel better in a minute.'

But she very much doubted that she would. Not when he called her 'sweetheart' in that low, sexy voice of his. Nor was it easy to ignore the long, muscular thigh touching her own, and the movement of his hand as it slid very slowly up over her back. She shivered involuntarily at the soft pressure of his fingers, only gradually relaxing as he began to gently massage the tense muscles at the nape of her neck.

Beneath his magic touch she could practically feel the stress and strain leaching away from her weary body. And, despite telling herself that she must be stark, staring mad to let this man anywhere near her, she couldn't seem to find the will or the energy to do anything about it. In fact, not only was the whole situation totally unreal somehow, but it must be the effect of the brandy, scorching through her veins, because she was feeling quite extraordinarily light-headed and mindless as well.

'Mmm . . .' she sighed, and then—as she told herself when thinking about the unfortunate incident later—she made the mistake of turning her head to glance at him. Startled by the hard, sensual expression on his tanned face, she couldn't seem to tear her gaze away from the glittering topaz lights in his green eyes, the message they conveyed suddenly causing her stomach to lurch with shock and sexual tension.

'No, Maxim!' she gasped, shivering despite the heat from the open fire at the touch of his hand moving up to pluck the combs from her hair. 'Please don't!' she begged, her own hands fluttering helplessly as the long, heavy mass of her hair tumbled down about her shoulders, and she seemed unable to prevent him from drawing her body slowly towards him.

He raised his other hand, winding his fingers through the curly tresses of her pale gold hair, holding her head firmly beneath him and tilting it back, so that she was forced to look up into his face. Her head seemed to be throbbing with a strange fever, her blue eyes widening in her pale face as she gazed up at the hard, sensual line of his mouth. She knew he was going to kiss her, but she couldn't move, trapped in a strange hypnotic trance by the intense, fiery gleam in his eyes. And then his mouth came down to take possession of hers, parting her lips and invading her mouth with ruthless determination. She moaned helplessly as he pushed her back against the cushions. His hands were sweeping over her body, his strong fingers erotically caressing her soft curves with a mounting, hungry passion which left her dazed and trembling in his arms.

His lips softened, moving over hers with a slow, languorous sensuality which provoked a wanton, passionate response in her quivering body which she was helpless to deny. She was consumed by a rushing tide of fierce pleasure and excitement; only aware of the strong arousal of the firm, hard body pressed so closely to her own, the increasingly rapid beating of his heart, and the scorching heat of his mouth. Almost of their own volition, her arms slowly closed about his neck, her fingers clinging to his thick, black hair as she feverishly responded to his kiss.

Slowly releasing her lips, he raised his head to stare down at her: at the sweet, trembling temptation of her lips and her fluttering eyelids as she gazed sightlessly back at him, totally in the thrall of a storm of passionate desire.

'Oh, Stephanie!' he groaned softly, burying his face in her hair for a moment. 'I must tell you that I . . .' But whatever else he might have been going to say was lost as the sudden, abrupt summons of a telephone crashed through their total absorption with one another.

It took them both some moments to realise exactly where they were, Maxim responding to the noisy, impatient ringing by swearing violently under his breath as he slowly removed his arms from about her trembling body.

He looks even more shattered than I feel, was her first coherent thought as she mentally struggled to pull herself together, watching with dazed eyes as Maxim reluctantly rose to his feet and began walking across the room.

'Yes?' he barked, lifting the receiver of the instrument on his desk. 'Oh—it's you,' he added, his harsh expression softening as he listened to the voice on the the other end of the telephone.

As she levered herself up from amid the rum-

pled cushions, harsh reality began to return with a
vengeance. A deep flush spread across her pale
features, before draining away again. She began to
shake so badly that she had to clasp her fingers
tightly together for a moment. It must be shock,
she thought wildly, forcing her trembling hands to
smooth down the dress which had ridden up
about her thighs.

Dear heaven, what *had* she been doing?
Stephanie almost groaned aloud as she realised
how her weak body had betrayed her yet again!
What was she going to do? He'd be off that damn
telephone in a minute—and then what? How on
earth was she going to explain away her behaviour
when she didn't even begin to understand it
herself?

It was practically impossible to concentrate on
the urgent problem when her body was still
throbbing like a drum. Maxim's kiss had roused
her senses to such a pitch that every nerve of her
being seemed to be crying out for sexual satisfaction.

Desperately hunting for her combs, she hardly
heard what he was saying on the phone, but
distraught as she was she couldn't help but notice
his occasional smile, and the warmth of his voice
as he talked to the caller. It was bound to be a
woman on the other end of the line. And why not?
she thought grimly, trembling with self-disgust.
She was, after all, just one of a long string of
females who, if they'd all capitulated as easily as
she had done, would undoubtedly keep him

happily occupied well into the next century.

Maxim finally put down the receiver and turned towards her. 'I'm sorry about that.' He shrugged. 'It was just . . .'

'One of your girlfriends?' she hissed through clenched teeth.

'What?' His dark brows drew together in an impatient frown. 'That was Paul. My stepson,' he added, when she continued to gaze at him with a blank expression on her pale face.

'I didn't know——Oh, yes, I . . . I do remember you once saying something,' she murmured breathlessly, clinging to the safe, harmless subject of his son. 'How—er—how old is he now?'

'Twenty-three—and a bit of a problem at the moment,' Maxim replied. 'He wants to become a professional musician, and I'm not too happy about that. Although I have to admit that he's a very talented flautist—or so I've been told.'

'Well, if that's what he wants to do, maybe you should let him have a go at it,' she muttered, her fingers still probing amongst the cushions. It seemed as though Maxim, too, was regarding his stepson as a safe topic of conversation. If she could just keep him talking, *and* find those damn hair combs of hers—she might be able to get out of the house, and this very embarrassing situation, with a few shreds of dignity.

'Unfortunately, it's not as easy as that,' he was saying. 'Paul is due to inherit a large financial empire, and I promised his mother that . . .' He clamped his lips together abruptly as her eyes flew to his face. She saw a muscle beating in his clenched jaw before she quickly tore her gaze away from his rigid figure.

The whole situation suddenly became too much for her to cope with any longer. 'I . . . I can't find my combs,' she wailed helplessly, feeling certain that she was going to burst into a flood of humiliating tears any minute.

'You look fine as you are,' Maxim said soothingly as he came forward, retrieving the errant objects from beneath a cushion and placing them in her shaking hands. 'I'll just go and get your coat, and order my car to be brought around to the front door,' he added quietly. 'That will give you a few moments to fix yourself up before I take you home, hmm?'

Stephanie could only bless the comforting darkness of the night as he ushered her into his red Ferrari sports car a few minutes later. She'd done what she could about her bedraggled appearance, but she knew that the sum total of the day's emotional shocks had taken a dire toll, leaving her feeling, and looking, like a worn-out dishrag.

He started the car and drove silently down the long gravelled drive. It wasn't until they had almost reached the lodge and the imposing, ornamental iron gates that marked the entrance of the house and the estate, that he gave a heavy sigh and said, 'I'm sorry, Stephanie.'

'So I should hope!' she snapped. 'Kissing me like that, and . . .'

'Oh no!' He gave a low, sensual laugh that sent

shivers down her backbone. 'I have *no* intention of apologising for kissing you. My only regret is that we were interrupted by that phone call.'

'You're disgusting!'

'Am I?' he laughed again. 'How strange—I don't recall you being particularly disgusted at the time. In fact, now I come to think about it, your response was really quite . . .'

'Oh, *shut up!*' she ground out angrily, raising a trembling hand to her hot, flushed cheeks.

No more was said by either of them for a while as he drove through the open gates and turned into the road which led to the village.

'OK, let's start again,' Maxim said, breaking the tense silence. 'When I said I was sorry, I was referring to the disruption which our—er—reunion has caused in your life. I'm genuinely sorry about that.'

'Wow—big deal!'

'And I am not going to pretend that it's an easy situation for either of us,' he added, ignoring her sarcastic comment. 'Because quite clearly it isn't.'

'You can say that again!'

He sighed impatiently. 'I do wish you'd stop this pointless sniping. It isn't going to achieve anything, is it?' He paused for a moment, and when she remained silent, he continued, 'I'm quite sure that with a modicum of tolerance and good will we can smooth matters out between us.'

'And no prizes for guessing just *who* is expected to be "tolerant" and brimming over with "good will",' she muttered gloomily.

'Oh, I don't know . . .' he murmured, driving slowly down the dimly lit village street. 'I'd say that I've shown remarkable tolerance regarding your boyfriend, for instance.'

Stephanie turned to stare at the hard, chiselled lines of his profile, her mind in a whirl of confusion. 'What boyfriend?'

'I'm referring to that blond-haired Lothario of yours,' he drawled with cool amusement. 'The man you were kissing so passionately outside your shop earlier this afternoon.'

'Do you mean Guy?' She gazed at him in blank astonishment, until she realised that Maxim must have been looking out of the apartment window above the shop when she had returned from her lunch date with Guy. 'But I wasn't . . . I mean . . .'

'I'm not concerned about the details of that—or any other relationship you may have had in the past,' he remarked flatly as he drew up outside her house.

'I should think not!'

He shrugged. 'However, as Adam's father, I now have a vested interest as far as your future conduct is concerned . . .'

'My *conduct*?'

'. . . and I'm not prepared to allow that sort of behaviour to continue.'

Stephanie gasped, her mouth opening and closing like a fish as she tried to comprehend the full extent of his extraordinary statement. Never in all her life had she ever heard anything so preposterous! And from Maxim, *of all people!* Surely he must be kidding? Yes, of course he was!

'Look, I know you think you're being funny——'
she began. And then, with the aid of the
moonlight shining in through the car windows,
she caught the chilly gleam in his green eyes. She
began to realise—totally absurd and far-fetched as
it might seem—that he was in deadly earnest. 'I
simply don't believe this. You—you *must* be
joking!' she exclaimed, her voice shrill with
incredulity.

'No.' The lazy mockery had evaporated from his
voice as if it had never existed. 'I expect you, as
Adam's mother, to be like Caesar's wife—above
suspicion.'

'You've got a nerve—you . . . you bloody man!'
she shouted, delving into the depths of her purse
for her house keys. 'Oh, I *really* hate these low-
slung, macho sports cars,' she added savagely,
wrestling with her safety-belt as Maxim got out
and came around to open the passenger door. 'Let
me tell you, I'll see who I like, when I like, and
there's not a damn thing you can do about it!'

'Oh, yes, there is, sweetheart,' he murmured,
calmly helping her out of the car and taking the
keys from her trembling hands. 'I can go to the
courts and claim custody of Adam.'

'You . . . you wouldn't!' she gasped, almost
running to keep up with him as he strode up the
path towards her front door.

He placed the key in the lock and opened the
door before turning towards her. 'Of course I
wouldn't, he drawled smoothly, raising his hand

to run a long, slim finger down her pale cheek. 'Just as long as you do as I say, and get rid of your blond boyfriend.'

'But I can't do that,' she exploded. 'He's my accountant, for heaven's sake!'

Maxim shrugged. 'Too bad. You'll just have to find another one, won't you?'

The lines of his face might be stern and inflexible, but she was perfectly well aware of the hard, sardonic gleam in the depths of his green eyes; and Stephanie knew, for the first time in her life, just what it was that drove some people to commit murder.

'I'm not giving into this . . . this blackmail!' she shouted angrily. 'And certainly not from a two-timing rat like yourself!' she added, quickly stepping into the hall and slamming the door shut in his face. Leaning panting against the old oak door, she listened to the sound of his car as Maxim drove away, feeling as if her head was going to burst with rage at any minute. She wanted to scream and scream, and go on screaming until the little men in white coats came and removed her to a quiet, peaceful asylum—miles and miles away from the appalling, horrific nightmare which her life had suddenly become.

CHAPTER SIX

STEPHANIE sighed with pleasure as the soaring notes of the leading violin led the other members of the chamber orchestra into the first movement of *La Primavera*, from Vivaldi's *The Four Seasons*. Closing her eyes and leaning back in her seat, she slowly began to relax beneath the soothing effect of the beautiful music.

She hadn't been mad about attending this concert tonight. After the exhaustion of the last few days, she had been longing to soak her weary limbs in a hot, steamy bath, followed by the blessed comfort of bed—and sleep. However, not wanting to disappoint Guy, she'd forced herself to dash home, shower and change into a black silk dress, and be ready to greet her accountant with a tired smile when he had called to collect her. After all, it was the least she could do, especially when he had gone to such trouble to obtain the concert tickets.

And wasn't it also a perfect opportunity to show Maxim that you weren't going to give in to his blackmail? queried a small, internal voice.

Nonsense! Even Maxim could hardly object to her attending a concert, especially one held in the very public surroundings of the Georgian Assembly Room in Cheltenham.

Oh, no? Who are you kidding?, the voice retorted.

Was that a hollow laugh, competing with the strings of the orchestra as it echoed weirdly in her brain? Well, just at the moment she was too tired and fed up to care *what* Maxim thought—or what he might do. It was all right for him! Financial tycoons didn't have to worry or bother about the minutiae of everyday life. Dwelling in isolation on the top floor of their modern office blocks, they were wrapped in protective cotton wool, with attentive PAs and secretaries only too anxious to cater for their every whim. What did they know—or care—about the trials and tribulations of lesser mortals? They should try working as a self-employed single parent for a few days. That would certainly bring them down to earth, she thought grimly.

Although she'd hardly had a wink of sleep after that disastrous dinner with Maxim, tossing and turning throughout the night, she'd had no choice but to drag herself wearily into the shop the next morning. From thereon she seemed to have been trapped on a roller-coaster—and travelling strictly downhill all the way.

The first problem had been the reason for Lisa's late arrival.

'I can't stay long, love,' she had said breathlessly as she'd rushed into the shop. 'Katy has gone down with the flu, I'm afraid. There seems to be quite an epidemic at the moment. I've got a friend keeping an eye on her for a while, but I'll have to get back to the poor little mite as soon as I can.'

Stephanie was immediately sympathetic about her assistant's predicament in trying to cope with her small seven year-old daughter. Like all single parents who worked for their living, she knew how very upsetting a child's illness could be. And not just because of the logistical problems involved. Far more difficult to cope with, in many ways, were the underlying feelings of guilt and self-reproach at not being able to be in two places at once. Despite all logic and common sense, working mothers of small children were only too apt to secretly blame themselves—however unfairly—for not being full-time housewives. It was a 'no win' situation, and Stephanie hastened to reassure her assistant.

'There's absolutely no need to worry. I can easily cope here on my own.'

The other woman sighed with relief. 'I was worried about letting you down, but—well . . .'

'Go back home and see to Katy,' Stephanie said firmly.

'I've got a sitter lined up for tomorrow, so I'll definitely be here on the dot of nine o'clock,' were the other woman's parting words as she hurriedly left the shop. But when Stephanie was woken next morning by the ringing of the telephone by her bed, and heard her assistant's thin, reedy voice, she knew that Lisa wouldn't be able to keep her promise.

'It sounds as if you've gone down with the same bug as Katy. How are you feeling?'

'Like death!' Lisa moaned. 'I'm so sorry about this, Stephanie. I've stuffed myself full of aspirins, but they don't seem to make the slightest difference.'

'Never mind. Stay home and keep warm. And don't even think of coming back until you're feeling better, OK?'

It really did appear as though there was an epidemic of influenza sweeping through the Cotswolds. Her telephone hardly seemed to stop ringing, with one after another of the home knitters she employed all calling the shop to say that they'd had to put down their knitting needles, and take to their beds. By the end of the next day, it was beginning to look as if well over half her outworkers were ill—and she wasn't feeling too good, either.

'The show must go on,' she'd told herself bracingly this morning, shivering and shaking as she'd driven in to work. Of course, it wouldn't be a total disaster if the shop did close for a day or two. But she had always tried to keep open, despite all adversity, and she was damned if she was going to give in to a few pesky germs!

All the same, she had felt no compunction about leaving earlier than usual this afternoon, and after fortifying herself with a glass of hot lemon juice—liberally topped up with a large slug of whisky—she'd felt able to manage the concert this evening. Only, sitting here now, and feeling like death warmed up, maybe it *hadn't* been such a good idea, after all . . .

As the glorious music filled the elegant room, she turned her head slightly to glance at Guy's profile. He really was such a very nice, kind and decent man. If *only* she could have fallen in love with him, and lived happily ever after. Why was it that one's heart never seemed to listen to the good, practical common-sense arguments put forward by one's brain? And what was it about a man like Maxim which apparently made him so irresistibly attractive to women?' As far as she could see, he had none of Guy's sterling virtues, such as trustworthiness and fidelity. And words like 'compassion' and 'tender-hearted' certainly weren't those associated with Maxim's hard, tough personality.

So how come she was still in love with him?

Over the past few days, and sleepless nights, she had been forced to acknowledge that her feelings for Maxim were the same as they had always been. Despite his despicable behaviour towards her in the past, and the intervening years during which she had thought she'd recovered from his evil spell, nothing it seemed could alter the love she still had for the man who had so cruelly betrayed her. How could she be such an idiot? she asked herself incredulously for the umpteenth time. A question to which—as always—she could find no logical or reasonable answer.

With a deep, inward sigh she tried to empty her mind and concentrate on the music. But it was proving impossible to ignore all the problems which seemed to be piling up on her frail shoul-

ders. The situation was a complete can of worms!
Despite the way Maxim had kissed her the other
night, she knew it had meant nothing to him. He
might . . . well, yes, he obviously did still find her
attractive, but that was just sex rearing its ugly
head again, even after all these years. Besides,
compared to the possible complexities of his
relationship with Claire, that brief encounter on
the sofa in Maxim's study paled into insignifi-
cance.

Busy as she'd been over the past few days, she'd
tried ringing Claire in London—but hadn't yet
managed to get hold to her. Her stepdaughter
hardly seemed to be spending any time at the
house which she shared with some friends in
Fulham, although she still had absolutely no idea
of what she would have said if the girl had
answered the phone. Dire warnings about Maxim
would mean having to tell Claire all about her past
love affair, and the fact that Adam wasn't her
brother; while at the same time she was leaving
herself wide open to the charge that she was
jealous of her stepdaughter——And could she
categorically deny that accusation?

There was something so truly awful about the
situation, that she had done her best not to think
about it. There was no blood tie between her stepdaughter and herself, but she loved Claire as if
she'd been her own child—despite the fact that
there was only eight years between them. So how
on earth was she going to cope with this macabre,
dreadful mess in which she and her stepdaughter

both appeared to be in love with the same man?

Stephanie wriggled uncomfortably in her seat. The whole situation was rapidly becoming like one of those fiendish Chinese puzzles—the more one unravelled them, the more complicated they became. It was all Maxim's fault, she told herself bitterly. And as for his crazy order that she should stop seeing Guy . . . Anyone would think she was a scarlet woman, for heaven's sake! As if her friendship with her accountant could possibly be construed as anything other than perfectly proper. Maxim clearly had a mind like a sewer. But love him or hate him—and the two emotions seemed to be inextricably bound together as far as she was concerned—she knew that she would never be free of the spell he had cast over her, all those years ago.

The strains of the final *allegro* slowly died away, and Stephanie sat up as the audience burst into enthusiastic clapping.

'Have you enjoyed yourself?' Guy asked, forced to raise his voice over the applause.

'Hmm, it was lovely,' she said, feeling momentarily ashamed that she had been so immersed in her own dismal thoughts that she had missed large sections of the performance.

'I've booked a table for dinner at La Ciboulette,' Guy was saying as they left the building, pausing for a moment as the crowd eddied about them.

At the mention of food, Stephanie felt her stomach give a sickening lurch. 'I . . . I'd rather not have anything to eat, if you don't mind. I'm honestly not feeling too well.'

'You don't look too good, either.' Guy gazed down at her pale face with concern. 'Don't worry, I'll take you straight home. I hope you're not going down with the flu virus which seems to have decimated half the county?'

'Oh, lord—so do I!' she prayed fervently as he took her arm and led her towards his car. Apart from trying to run the business single-handedly, she was going to have to stay on her feet, because it was the end of term at Adam's school, and she was due to collect him tomorrow morning.

Thanks to the fierce warmth of the heater in Guy's car, Stephanie had almost fallen asleep by the time they arrived back at the house. Even Guy's envious comment, 'Gosh—I'd give my eye teeth for a sports car like that!' failed to warn her of danger. It was only when Guy came around to open the passenger door of his vehicle, and she looked across the moonlit forecourt to see Maxim getting out of his red Ferrari, that she was alerted to the disastrous scenario about to break over her head.

'Ah, there you are at last, darling,' Maxim drawled smoothly.

Stephanie gazed at him in horror. 'What . . . what are you doing here?' she asked, shaking her head in confusion, and trying to clear the mists from her sleepy brain.

'Well, *darling* . . .' Maxim said smoothly, once again putting a heavy, sardonic emphasis on the

endearment. 'I was wondering where you'd got
to. Why you'd stood me up like this.'

'Stood you up?' Stephanie blinked and shook
her dazed head again. 'But I didn't. I . . .'

'Mrs Hammond and I have been to a concert,'
explained Guy, reluctantly taking his eyes off the
long, sleek sports car to eye Maxim up and
down. 'In Cheltenham, actually,' he added
pompously, clearly not liking what he saw.

'Have you *actually* been to Cheltenham,
darling?' Maxim drawled, in a cruel parody of
Guy's English accent. 'But what about our
dinner date?'

'What dinner date?' Stephanie looked at him
with rising fury. 'You know damn well . . .'

'She's always doing this to me.' Maxim turned
to Guy with a shrug. 'You know how it is with
these sort of women—always playing fast and
loose with us poor men.'

'No, I . . . I can't say I do,' Guy muttered,
clearly out of his depth and bewildered by the
whole affair.

Stephanie stamped her foot with fury. 'Look,
this is all quite ridiculous!' she told Maxim. 'Will
you kindly go away?'

'Why should I?' Maxim retorted, leaning
casually against his car. 'I've had a long, hard
week toiling away in London, and all I've had to
look forward to was the thought of your nice,
warm bed waiting for me tonight.'

'You lying bastard!'

Maxim turned to Guy. 'Is she like this with you?

Or am I the only poor sucker to get this rough treatment?' he asked the other man in an aggrieved voice.

'No, I . . . er . . .' Guy fingered his tie nervously, the Englishman's horror of being involved in an emotional scene clearly etched on his face. 'I—I'm sorry, Stephanie, I had no idea that you had—er—a prior engagement.'

'Of course I haven't,' she cried. 'It's all nonsense!'

'Oh, darling! How can you say that?' Maxim murmured, his voice throbbing with false sincerity as he walked over to take hold of her arm. 'And especially after all we've meant to each other?'

'Let go of me, you foul man!' she stormed, trying to wriggle away from his firm grip. 'You mustn't listen to him, Guy, he's just making up this nonsense.'

Her accountant gave a nervous cough. 'Yes, well, I—um—I think I'd better be getting along,' he said, edging away from her struggling figure.

'Yes, you do that, old chap—toodle-oo!' Maxim said in another dreadful imitation of Guy's accent.

'I'll kill you, Maxim, I really will!' she ground out savagely, and tried to turn towards Guy to explain that Maxim was lying his head off. But before she could do so she found herself being swung quickly around into his arms, which closed tightly about her. A brief second later he had ruthlessly possessed her lips in a kiss of devastating intensity.

Kicking his shins and pummelling her fists upon his broad shoulders had no effect whatsoever, and it wasn't until the sound of Guy's car was fading away in the distance that he eventually let her go.

'How . . . how can you do this to me?' she gasped, and would have fallen if he hadn't kept a firm grip on her arm as he led her weak, trembling figure towards the front door. 'We only went to a concert, for heaven's sake!'

'I told you to get rid of that man,' Maxim said calmly, taking hold of her bag, extracting the keys and smoothly opening the door. 'And since you clearly had no intention of doing so, I decided to take action.'

Stephanie stamped angrily into the house. 'Well, I hope you're pleased with yourself!'

'When you calm down, you'll see that I've done you a favour,' he said with a maddening, sardonic grin. 'That man was obviously spineless—a total wimp!'

The fact that she had unfortunately come to the same gloomy conclusion did nothing to cool her temper. 'You really don't understand, do you?' she raged. 'Thanks to you, I'm not just going to need a new accountant, you've also destroyed my good name. In fact, by the time Guy's had a few drinks in his local pub, my reputation will have just about hit zero. Thanks a bunch—*darling*!'

'Hey—relax,' he murmured.

'And it isn't just my problem,' she grated. 'Most of Adam's schoolmates live around Broadway. So it's even money—once the gossip begins going

around that I'm a loose woman—that he's going to
hear about it as well. But why should you worry?'
she added viciously. 'You've had your fun for the
evening—right?'

Maxim's dark brows drew together in a heavy
frown. 'Oh, come on, there's no need to exagger-
ate,' he murmured. 'Why don't we discuss this
quietly over a cup of coffee?'

'For heaven's sake, this isn't New York!'
Stephanie burst out. 'You simply don't have a clue
about rural English life, do you?' she added with a
heavy sigh, suddenly feeling deathly tired and
exhausted. 'And no, I'm certainly *not* going to give
you a cup of coffee. In fact, if you're not off my
property in five seconds flat—I'm going to call the
police!'

A moment later the door was slammed shut in
his face. Walking slowly back to his car, Maxim
paused for few minutes, buried deep in thought as
he stared blindly into the hazy darkness before
getting into his Ferrari and driving away.

Some time in the very early hours of the next
morning, Stephanie woke from a hideous dream.
Her body felt as if it was on fire, and yet her slim
frame was racked by icy cold shivers that made her
teeth clatter uncontrollably. It was unbearably
painful to move her head, which pounded and
throbbed as if someone was banging a sledge
hammer against her skull, obliterating all thought
except the driving need to gain relief from such
torture. Stumbling out of bed, she managed to

stagger into her bathroom, wincing at the sharp,
stabbing pain in her eyes as she switched on the
light to hunt through the medicine cupboard for
some aspirins.

Slipping back into bed again, her body shivering
in the grip of a violent fever, she was deeply
ashamed to find herself giving way to a storm of
tears. Maybe if she wasn't feeling so rotten, she'd
have been able to face the loss of everything she'd
built up over the years. But she now knew that she
had no choice but to move from the area. There
was no certainty that Guy would keep his mouth
shut about what had happened tonight. And,
even if he told just one of his many friends, the
image which Maxim had painted of her—that of a
loose, immoral woman—would soon leak out in
such a small, rural community.

Alternatively gasping from the raging heat and
shaking violently beneath the freezing, icy shivers
which racked her body, the night seemed endless.
Stephanie knew she must have slipped into a fitful
doze from time to time, but when she eventually
awoke she didn't feel as if she'd had a wink of
sleep. Her body was drenched in sweat, every
bone and muscle aching as she continued to shiver
and shake with fever.

Although she'd put up a valiant fight, and kept
on working as long as she could, it was now
obvious that she had fallen a victim to the current
flu epidemic. And, even if she couldn't possibly
open the shop today, she knew that she must get
up. Because, however ill she might be feeling—

and, like Lisa, she felt as though she definitely had
one foot in the grave—she still had to fetch Adam
from school.

By the time she had eased her aching, trembling
body into a pair of warm slacks and a heavy
sweater, Stephanie felt totally drained and
exhausted. Pulling aside the curtains, she saw that
it was pouring with rain. That's all I need! she
thought listlessly, before glancing at the clock on
her bedside table, and realising that she would
have to get a move on. Since it was a Saturday,
and Tilly only worked for her during the week, she
really ought to try and prepare lunch for Adam
before going off to collect him from school.

Careful to move slowly, so as not to jar her pain-
fully throbbing head, she forced her weak, trembling legs across the floor and out on to the landing.

Clinging dizzily to the banister, she was slowly
making her way down the stairs when she was
startled by the loud ringing of the front door bell.
Raising her head to look out through the window
over the door, she stiffened with shock and alarm.

'Oh, *no*!' she gasped, her dazed eyes widening
at the sight of the long, thoroughbred lines of a red
sports car parked in front of the house.

The doorbell sounded again imperiously, and
Stephanie shivered, her body taut with nervous
tension. What on earth was Maxim doing here?
There was no way she could possibly cope with
him—not the way she was feeling this morning.

The bell stopped ringing, but any hope that she
was going to be left in peace and quiet proved

shortlived. Maxim was now banging on the oak door, the rising crescendo of sound competing with the headache already pounding in her head until she couldn't take any more.

'All right,' she called out wearily. 'I'm coming.'

By the time she had managed to navigate the remainder of the stairs, she had reached such a pitch of exhaustion that she didn't care if it was the devil himself at the door—just as long as she could somehow stop that infernal noise.

As she unfastened the latch, the door was pushed determinedly open, the movement sending her tottering backwards against the wall as Maxim walked in.

He slammed the door behind him, and stood regarding her with a grim expression on his face as he shook out his wet trenchcoat. 'I thought you were never going to let me in. Or were you intending to leave me out in the rain?' Stephanie raised a shaking hand to her throat. 'W-what are you doing here?' she croaked, shivering from the draught in the hall, vaguely noting that this was the first time she'd seen him in anything other than a formal suit as she gazed at his tall figure, clothed in beige cord trousers and a matching soft cashmere sweater over a casual checked shirt.

'I've come to apologise for my behaviour last night,' he said, staring intently down at her as he shrugged off his wet coat. 'There isn't much light here in the hall, but you look very pale. Are you feeling OK?'

'Yes, I'm fine. In fact I'm just about to collect

Adam from his school,' she replied, trying to
sound bright and confident, but spoiling the effect
as she quickly grabbed hold of of the hall table to
prevent her wobbly legs from giving way beneath
her.

'You seem very far from "fine",' he said flatly,
putting an arm about her waist and leading her
into the warm, bright kitchen, where he pulled out
a chair from the table and helped her to sit down.

Stephanie leaned back and closed her eyes for a
moment. She knew he was staring down at her,
and that she must look a fright, but she was feeling
too ill to care.

Maxim's lips tightened, his dark brows coming
together in a frown as he gazed at the girl slumped
in the chair. She was very pale, her skin waxen,
the non-colour of her ash-blonde hair emphasising
the weary fragility of her features. 'I was right, you
don't look well. In fact, you look terrible,' he
added with brutal honesty.

'Th—thanks!' she ground out.

'It's obvious that you're running a high temperature,' he said, ignoring her feeble efforts to
dissuade him as he placed a cool hand on her
forehead.

Stephanie sighed heavily. Dazed and shaking
with fever, she was feeling too exhausted to put up
any more of a fight.

'Yes, well . . .' She sighed again. 'I reckon I must
have got the flu. Everybody else has, so I guess it's
my turn,' she muttered through teeth which
clattered like castanets. 'And if you've got any

sense, you get yourself out of here before you catch it, too.'

Maxim gave a wry, sardonic laugh. 'Ah—but I never did have any sense, not where you were concerned,' he murmured, bending down to scoop her up in his strong arms.

'What do you think you're d-doing?' she gasped hoarsely. 'Put me down at once!'

Ignoring her breathless protest, he carried her across the kitchen. 'I'm taking you to where you belong—back to bed.'

'This is ridiculous!' she exclaimed huskily.

'Not half as ridiculous as thinking you're well enough to fetch Adam from school, you stupid girl!' he grated harshly as he began to mount the stairs.

He had no right to talk to her like that, Stephanie thought indignantly, knowing that she ought to be putting up at least some resistance. But her body was shivering so uncontrollably, her senses bemused by the tantalising, musky scent of his cologne and the sight of the tanned skin of his cheek, only inches away from her own face, that she lay meekly in his arms until he reached the landing.

'OK—where do we go from here?' he demanded, and when she waved a hand towards an open door he carried her through into her bedroom, laying her gently down on the bed.

'Look, I . . . I don't want you to think I'm not grateful, but I really can't stay up here,' she muttered hoarsely, struggling to sit up. 'It's the end of term, and I've got to collect Adam and all his luggage, and . . .'

Maxim sat down on the bed beside her, putting his hands on her shoulders and gently pressing her back against the pillows. 'You're not going anywhere. Apart from anything else, you're obviously not in a fit state to drive a car.'

'The school isn't very far away,' she croaked, trembling nervously at the touch of his warm fingers as he leaned forward to brush the damp tendrils of hair from her brow.

Maxim frowned and shook his head. 'I don't care if it's just around the corner. You're not going —and that's that!'

'But what about Adam?' she wailed helplessly.

'I'm perfectly capable of picking the boy up for you,' he said, ignoring her protests as he fetched a cold facecloth from the bathroom, and placed it on her burning forehead. 'There's no need to worry. I give you my word that I won't say anything to Adam—other than the fact that, as an old friend of yours, I'm helping you out in your hour of need. All of which is absolutely true, hmm?'

'Yes, but . . .'

'Besides, I don't imagine that boys have changed very much since my day,' he grinned. 'So you can bet your bottom dollar that he's going to enjoy a ride in my car!'

Yes, he was quite right, she told herself miserably, trying to suppress a sudden pang of jealousy. Adam would be absolutely thrilled at the opportunity of travelling in the fast sports car. And since

Maxim had promised not to say anything about their previous relationship, and she clearly wasn't able to drive over to the school herself, there didn't seem to be a thing she could do about it.

'OK, now let's get some aspirins into you,' he said, passing her the tablets and a glass of water before adding, 'And then we'll have those clothes off.'

'What?' she gasped, choking and spluttering as she stared up at him in alarm and confusion.

'I'm not leaving here until you're undressed and tucked up in bed,' he told her firmly.

'No! Please . . . there's no need. I can m-manage,' she stammered huskily, her cheeks flushing a deep red as Maxim proceeded to take not a blind bit of notice of her breathless protests; quickly and efficiently stripping her slacks, the heavy sweater and her underclothes from her helpless, trembling body.

'That's a good girl,' he murmured, easing a fresh silk nightgown over her full breasts, and pulling it down to cover her smooth, bare thighs.

'I'll n-never forgive you!' she moaned bitterly, wrapping her arms about her shivering figure, which was shaking as much with rage as much as with fever.

'Oh, yes, you will,' he drawled, and she shivered at the faint mockery in his voice as he pulled up the sheet and smoothed the blankets over her rigid figure.

To her utter consternation, there didn't seem to be anything Stephanie could do to prevent her eyes from filling with weak tears.

'Ah, sweetheart, there's no need to cry,' Maxim murmured softly as he sat down on the bed beside her. 'I couldn't just leave you here, not without trying to make you more comfortable before I left to get Adam from school.'

He leaned forward, gently wiping the tears from her eyes with one of his large handkerchiefs, his tanned, handsome face so close to her own that she could feel his breath caressing her cheek. And then he lowered his head a fraction, brushing his lips softly across her damp eyelids, and down over a pale cheek towards her trembling mouth, the touch of his lips moving over hers almost beguiling in its gentleness.

She tried to close her mind to the devastating pleasure of his kiss, but it wasn't her mind that he was affecting, and it seemed that her body—weak and ill though it was—had a will of its own. A sudden insidious heat, which had nothing to do with her feverish temperature, flooded through her quivering figure; a hot wave of desire against which she had no defence.

'Please, Maxim!' she gasped, finally managing to turn her head away. 'I'm sorry . . . I mean, I really am grateful to you for . . . for offering to pick up Adam.'

'It will be a pleasure,' he said, warmth and tenderness softening the formal politeness of his words as he smiled gently down at her flushed face. 'And I still haven't told you how sorry I am about last night. Believe me, I had *no* idea that I would be endangering your reputation, and I do most sincerely want to apologise.'

Stephanie blinked. She was feeling so rotten that she knew she really wasn't thinking straight, but surely it wasn't like Maxim to be doing the 'humble apology' bit?

'That's all right,' she mumbled. 'I'd already more or less made up my mind that I was going to have to . . .'

'No,' he said, interrupting her firmly. 'I've caused a problem, and so I must put matters straight. In fact, the solution is blindingly clear. We must get married—immediately.'

'*Married?*' she exclaimed huskily. 'You and *me*?' She lifted a shaky, trembling hand to her hot, damp forehead. 'Are you saying that you want to marry *me*?'

Maxim raised a dark eyebrow. 'Of course. Who else would I have in mind? Besides which, it has to be the obvious answer to all your problems,' he told her firmly. 'There won't be any nonsense about your "reputation"—not when you're married to me,' he added, a note of hard, flat determination in his voice. 'Not only do you clearly need a man around the house but, more importantly, Adam needs a father. I'm sure we're both agreed that, where possible, children need a secure and stable background, right?'

'Yes, I . . . I suppose so,' she muttered, still feeling dazed and confused as she tried to come to terms with what he was suggesting.

'I know so,' he said firmly. 'And since we're

both free, and well over the age of twenty-one, it seems to be the least we can do for our son. Surely you must see that?'

'But what . . . what about Claire?' she queried, a deep flush creeping up over her pale cheeks.

'That's no problem,' he said dismissively.

'What?'

He shrugged. 'Claire understands the situation.'

Stephanie tried to sit up, her eyes widening as she gazed at him with bewilderment. 'She does?'

'Sure she does. I know she's disappointed at having to give up her job, but . . .'

'So, you're just planning to dump her, huh?'

'Of course I'm not,' he retorted coldly.

'Well, it sure sounds like it to me!' Stephanie gasped, falling back exhausted against the pillows. How could he possibly bring himself to act towards her sweet, lovely stepdaughter in such a dastardly manner?

'It's hardly the end of the world if Claire has to find another job, now is it?' he shrugged.

'You really are the pits!' Stephanie exclaimed incredulously. 'How can you possibly treat her like that?'

Maxim raised a dark eyebrow. 'Oh, come on! The new firm for whom Claire will be working are going to double her salary. Besides which, it's a step up in her career, which can't be bad.'

'Well, I reckon I've heard it all now!' Stephanie shook her head in bemusement, her eyes glazed with fatigue. One of us *has* to be out of our tiny minds! she thought wearily, suddenly feeling totally worn out and exhausted by the whole, extraordinarily bizarre situation.

'Well?'

'Hmm?'

He gave a short bark of rueful laughter. 'It may have escaped your attention, but I was under the impression that I'd just proposed to you!'

'I'm sorry, Maxim, but I'm just feeling too ill to cope with this at the moment . . .' she muttered, her eyes closing wearily.

'Oh, sweetheart, I'm sorry. I guess I should have waited until you're feeling stronger,' he said, gazing down with concern at her pale, limp figure. 'I'll be back soon with Adam,' he said, putting a fresh glass of water on her bedside table. 'In the meantime, try and go to sleep. I promise you that you'll feel better soon,' he murmured, and she felt the soft brush of his mouth across her trembling lips.

When Stephanie opened her eyes again, it was to see the bedroom door closing quietly behind his tall figure. With a muffled sob, she turned over and buried her face in the pillows, her slim body racked with bitter, miserably unhappy tears.

CHAPTER SEVEN

WRAPPED in shawls and blankets, Stephanie lay ensconced on a sofa by the log fire burning in the inglenook fireplace, looking out through the window at the rain teeming down outside in the garden. So much for April showers—it was more like the flood which launched Noah's ark, she thought, shivering slightly in her warm woollen dressing-gown and feeling thankful to be indoors on a day like this. But that was just about all she had to be thankful about. In fact, it was a long time since she'd felt quite so low and depressed as she did at this moment; a thick, heavy pall of gloom and doom, which obstinately refused to go away.

It was all Maxim's fault, of course, she told herself glumly. He'd virtually taken over her house—and her life—during the last week when she'd been so ill. Not only had he fixed for someone from an agency to run the shop until Lisa had been well enough to return, but he had also arranged for a professional nurse to care for her until she was well enough to get rid of the bossy woman who had been driving her up the wall. On top of which, there had also been a constant stream of delicious, appetising meals sent down from the manor house by Mrs Jenkins.

And yet, never once during the last week had he made any further reference to his extraordinary proposal of marriage. Or his quite astonishing statement that, as far as Claire was concerned, everything was definitely hunky-dory. She'd never heard of anything so amazingly weird and bizarre! Of course, she'd done her best to avoid giving him any opportunity to raise the matter. It was obviously some sort of tricky manoeuvre on Maxim's part—maybe to make it easier for him to get his hands on Adam?—and until she found an opportunity to have a long talk with Claire there was no point in even thinking about it. Or so she'd told herself—but in truth she had thought of little else, her emotions swaying her first one way and then another, leaving her dizzy with doubt and uncertainty.

However, the most depressing aspect of her illness had been Maxim himself. Everywhere she turned, there he was: tall, dark, impossibly handsome—and what was *really* making her see red was that he'd managed to fool everyone else into thinking that he was the greatest thing since sliced bread.

Lisa, fully recovered from the flu and now back, running the shop in Stephanie's absence, had immediately caved in to Maxim's charm.

'He's *so* attractive, and quite fantastically good-looking!' Lisa had sighed when she'd come over to see Stephanie a few days ago. 'Now that I know he's a widower—and rich as Croesus—maybe I'll start dieting again.'

'I thought you said no man was worth the effort of having to live on liver and orange juice?' Stephanie had muttered grumpily.

'Hmm . . . well, I think I could *just* make an exception in his case! Or maybe I might try that new diet I heard about the other day. How does the idea of nothing but freshly boiled tripe and yoghurt grab you? They say the weight just drops off. What do you think?'

'I'm not surprised!' Stephanie had declared grimly. 'Frankly, I think you must be crazy,' she'd added, looking at the other girl with exasperation as she realised that her normally down-to-earth, sensible assistant was afflicted with temporary insanity. And her housekeeper didn't seem to be in any better shape, either.

'Ooh . . . that Mr Tyler's such a lovely gentleman!' Tilly had said only yesterday. 'Fancy him buying the estate, and not knowing that you, being a distant cousin of his, was living here all the time.'

'Yes, just fancy,' Stephanie had muttered stonily. She was getting used to the fiction which Maxim had spread around the village while she was confined to bed, to account for his constant presence in the house. Unfortunately, by the time she had started to recover from the flu, it was too late for her to contradict his fairy story. The only merit in the whole farago of nonsense being that it did offer an explanation for the startling resemblance between Adam and Maxim.

However, Tilly's romantic old heart was clearly

beating overtime. 'Poor Mr Tyler, him being a lonely widower and all,' she'd said, pausing in her dusting to give Stephanie a speculative glance. 'Rattling around in that big house of his—it's plain to see that what he needs is a wife. And seeing as how Mr Tyler's taking such an interest in Adam, well, who knows what might happen?' she'd sighed hopefully.

Luckily Stephanie's sharp retort: 'Oh, for heaven's sake—why don't you mind your own business?' had so affronted the old woman that she'd stumped off in a huff, and hadn't—thank goodness—referred to the subject again.

Stephanie stared into the fire, depression hanging over her like a thick fog. She felt like crying all the time and she simply didn't know why. She knew she ought to be pleased that Adam and Maxim were getting on so well. And she was—only they weren't just getting on well, they were practically inseparable. Her son had quickly and easily succumbed to both Maxim's charm and the obvious interest he was taking in the boy. In fact, as far as Adam was concerned, Maxim was clearly the stuff of which heroes were made, and he had been clinging to their new neighbour as if to a shadow.

'The whole school were pea-green with envy when I left in that fantastic car,' he'd informed Stephanie as soon as Maxim had brought him back from school a week ago. 'Mr Tyler has said that I can use the large IBM computer he's got in his house, and he's promised to teach me how to write a program for it. I must say,' Adam had added reflectively, 'he does seem to be frightfully clever, and knows about a lot of things I've never even heard of.'

Dazed and feverish as she was, Stephanie had found herself smiling at the slight note of surprise in her son's voice. She loved Adam dearly, but there was no doubt that, although he was a clever little boy, it would do him no harm at all to be with someone who was, quite clearly, his intellectual superior. But that was the last time she had been able to smile about the situation. Because from that day forward it had seemed to her that she was, somehow, losing her son. She kept trying to tell herself that it was just her imagination. And although she tried not to be jealous Stephanie was frightened by the fast, rapid growth of the obvious rapport between Maxim and Adam, and hopelessly confused as to how to cope with it.

Her dismal thoughts were interrupted as Maxim came into the room, carrying a large bunch of cellophane-wrapped pink roses.

In one of those violent mood swings which seemed to have affected her lately, Stephanie suddenly felt ashamed of herself. She knew that she really ought to be grateful for all Maxim's care and attention. While she'd been so ill, he'd taken this last week off work, coming over to the house every day to see how she was, although it had been Adam whom he'd really come to see, of course. And yet, there again, how could she possibly object when Maxim had taken the boy out in his car to visit various museums and places of interest? Just as she hadn't felt able to protest at the amount of time he had spent with her son, just talking, reading or playing with the computers, either here or up at the manor house.

'These have just been delivered for you,' he said, placing the bouquet in her hands, before turning away to throw some more logs on the fire.

'Oh, how lovely,' she murmured, her cheeks flushing as she read the kind, loving message on the card. 'They—er—they're from Claire,' she added, not daring to look up at Maxim, her fingers trembling as she began to remove the wrapping. 'She really shouldn't have . . . I mean . . . this is the second bouquet she's sent me . . .'

'I know Claire wanted to have some time off work to come up and see you,' he drawled. 'But I'm afraid that I had to insist she remained in the office in London.'

I just bet you did! she thought savagely, knowing that the last thing he would want would be for the two women in his life to begin comparing notes; especially if he hadn't yet told Claire that he was Adam's father. In fact, even just thinking about all the various complications was enough to give anyone a raging headache. The loathsome man had so many balls in the air at once that maybe he should take up juggling for a profession, she thought grimly as he pulled up a chair and sat down beside her.

'I think it's about time we had a long talk, don't you?'

Noting the steely determination in his voice, Stephanie suddenly felt sick with tension. She glanced nervously at him through her eyelashes, noting the long length of his legs in the slim-fitting black cords and matching black cashmere sweater which emphasised his tan. With his black hair, he looked formidable, dangerous and—unfortunately —so diabolically attractive that it was all she could do to control herself as she struggled to fight an insane desire to leap into his arms.

'I don't think that . . .' Stephanie muttered, looking wildly around the room for inspiration. 'I wonder what's happened to Adam?'

'He's busy,' Maxim said, his lips twitching with amusement. 'In fact, when I left him up at the manor house just now, he informed me that he didn't wish to be disturbed for the next two hours. If I understood him correctly, I believe he's trying to hack in to the Bank of England computer!'

'Oh, lord, he won't succeed, will he?' she asked anxiously, her mind filled with images of her small son being carted off to prison, by either the police or members of the fraud squad.

Maxim laughed. 'No, of course not! However, just to be on the safe side, and since he's plugged in to the main terminal at my office, I've arranged for a member of the computer staff to keep an eye on him. And before you say anything,' he added quickly, 'I intend to give him a long, serious lecture about business ethics. Although, as the law stands at present, he isn't doing anything wrong— not unless he tries to steal any money.'

'All the same . . .'

'I quite agree. Adam mustn't be allowed to do it again. It was only because I was so certain that he won't succeed that I'm allowing him to play around with the computer. And also because I wanted to have a long, uninterrupted talk with you, of course.'

Stephanie gulped nervously. 'I . . . I've been meaning to thank you for being so—er—so kind to Adam,' she murmured, staring down at the hands tensely knotted in her lap.

'There's no need to thank me.' Maxim shrugged. 'Quite apart from the fact that he's my son, Adam is also very intelligent, and it's a pleasure to spend time with him.'

'Yes, well . . . thank you, all the same,' she muttered, feeling thoroughly miserable and unhappy. 'And also for spending so much time here, at the house.'

'Poor Stephanie,' he murmured lazily, putting out a hand to toy idly with a tendril of her long, blonde hair. 'Influenza is bad enough, but it often leaves people feeling low and depressed. That's how you feel at the moment, isn't it?'

'Mmm . . .' She nodded, careful not to look at him as her fingers plucked at the wool rug lying over her knees.

'Well, I'm obviously very sorry you've been so ill, but on the other hand, being able to spend so much time with Adam has given me the opportunity to get to know my son far better than I would have done normally.'

'I'm sure everyone must have guessed the truth by now,' she said gloomily.

'Guessed what?'

'About us and our . . . um . . . well, our past . . .' she hesitated, her cheeks reddening beneath the ironic gleam in his deep green eyes.

'You sound slightly confused,' he drawled. 'However, I imagine you must be referring to our love affair?'

The underlying, sardonic amusement in his voice struck a raw nerve. 'What "love affair"?' she queried scornfully. 'There's no point in either of us pretending that it was anything else but a brief, pathetically sordid relationship. Right?'

He lifted a dark, sardonic eyebrow. 'Is that what it was?'

'What else?' she demanded.

Maxim shrugged his broad shoulders. 'Well, if you say so,' he murmured blandly.

'Yes, I do,' she snapped, her anger and antagonism fuelled by his ready acceptance of her caustic words about their past relationship. Although why she should be suddenly feeling so miserably unhappy, when he had only confirmed what she'd always known to be the truth, she had absolutely no idea.

'However, we are straying from the point at issue, which seems to be your fear of local gossip. And I thought I'd already taken care of that, hmm?'

'Hah!' she snorted with derision. 'I don't think much of the "long-lost cousin" story you put out while I was ill.'

He shrugged. 'It was all I could think of at such short notice. However, it does touch on something I've been wanting to talk to you about.'

'About Adam, I suppose?' she muttered, leaning back against the cushions, suddenly feeling weary and exhausted.

'You're looking tired,' he commented, gazing at her pale face and the dark shadows under her blue eyes.

'Yes, I . . . I don't seem to have much energy these days,' she murmured, brushing a hand wearily through her hair.

'I've also noticed that you appear to be confused and disturbed—and maybe a little bit jealous—about the way Adam and I seem to be getting on so well, hmm?'

Her eyes flew to his face, but instead of the hard, ironic expression which she had expected she saw only warmth and concern. Such unexpected kindness was almost too much for her. 'Yes, I . . . I can't seem to help it,' she exclaimed helplessly, feeling all kinds of an idiot as her eyes filled with tears.

'It's perfectly natural,' he said softly, moving to sit on the sofa beside her, and pulling her trembling figure into his arms. 'You've had Adam to yourself for a long time now, and having to let someone else share even a part of your life together can't be easy. But that's not all, is it?'

'I don't know what you mean.' She sniffed and lifted a shaky hand to wipe the tears from her eyes.

'Well, just look at the life you lead,' he said, gently lifting the heavy curtain of her hair from her cheek. 'Trying to look after your child—as well as running a home, a shop and a knitting business— all on your own. That sort of existence can be very tough.'

She couldn't say anything. A heavy lump seemed to have formed in her throat, and the forbidden warmth and security of his embrace was almost tearing her apart.

'I've spoken about this before, but you were obviously too ill to think seriously about the matter,' he murmured, putting up a hand to her chin and slowly tilting her face up towards him. 'Not only can I take all those burdens off your shoulders, but it's obvious that what Adam needs is a permanent, full-time father.'

She gazed blindly up at him, all her senses in chaotic confusion as he ran a finger gently over her soft, trembling lips.

'And since it's the answer to so many of your problems, Stephanie, I really think that we should get married.'

'For . . . for Adam's sake?' she whispered huskily.

'Of course,' he drawled smoothly. 'You also seemed to be worried about Claire's reaction,' he added, his arms tightening about her as she tried to wriggle free of his embrace. 'And while I haven't, of course, said anything about the fact that we knew each other in the past, or that Adam is my son—I can tell you that I've already dis-

cussed the question of our marriage with Claire.
You'll be pleased to hear that she thoroughly
approves of the idea.'

'She does?' Stephanie gazed at him in astonishment for a moment, and then slowly shook her
head. 'I don't understand any of this,' she muttered helplessly, lying back exhausted in his arms.

'Poor Stephanie, you obviously still haven't fully
recovered from that damn virus. I guess I'd better
take you back to bed,' he said, rising from the sofa
and carrying her upstairs to her bedroom.

'I . . . I feel so low and depressed all the time,'
she muttered.

'I know. It's just the aftermath of the flu that's
making you feel so rotten,' he said soothingly, laying her carefully down on the bed before sitting
down on the mattress beside her. 'I won't press
you for an answer, not until you're ready to give it
to me.' He gently brushed aside the hair from her
brow. 'But there are other aspects of our marriage,'
he added, running his hand down her soft cheek.
'Other possible benefits that you might not have
considered . . .'

The warmth of his fingers as they slipped down
her neck and in under the opening of her dressing-
gown caused tremors of excitement to dance
across her skin. Tired and exhausted as she had
been a few moments ago, she could feel a heat
beginning to surge through her limbs as she stared
up at his face.

The kind concern which had been etched on his
features had evaporated, sponged away as though

it had never existed. There was now a hard, sensual angle to his features, the green eyes glittering beneath their heavy lids, the tanned skin stretched tautly over his cheekbones. She felt her own body knot in sudden tension as his fingers moved slowly and erotically down the deep valley between her breasts, barely covered by the thin silk nightdress beneath.

'Don't,' she muttered helplessly as he leaned towards her, her nostrils filled with the cool, astringent scent of his cologne, her slim figure trembling violently as his fingers slowly caressed the swollen fullness of her breasts, the rosy tips taut and aching for his touch. 'Maxim, please,' she whimpered. 'You . . . you're taking advantage of a sick woman!'

'Hmm, I know—shocking, isn't it?' he murmured sardonically as he pulled aside her dressing-gown, the few small buttons on her nightdress proving no obstacle to his questing fingers. She gasped, a low, husky groan breaking from her throat as his hands slipped down over her flesh before rising to cup her bare breasts, his fingers gently brushing over the hard, swollen points with such slow sensuality that she writhed and moaned in weak surrender to his masterly touch.

Maxim slowly and reluctantly withdrew his hands, and she opened her dazed eyes as he pulled the sides of her gown together to cover her nakedness. The fiery glitter in his eyes causing her heart to miss several beats.

'You see?' he murmured thickly. 'It isn't just

Adam. Our marriage could be very good for us as well. It would be a pity not to taste the sweetness of a full sexual relationship.'

Stephanie's body trembled with panic. Almost fainting with desire, she recognised the overwhelming temptation Maxim was offering, and it was all she could do not to break down and beg him to make love to her. Taking a deep, shuddering breath, she thrust his hands away and struggled to sit up against the pillows.

'No,' she whispered huskily. 'No, I can't . . . I . . .'

Maxim shrugged and rose slowly to his feet. 'Don't make the mistake of thinking that I'll allow you to marry anyone else,' he said coldly. 'When Adam's grown up, you can do what you like. But until that time, it's marriage to me—or to no one at all.'

Stephanie gasped. 'I've never heard anything so—so ridiculous. You can't possibly stop me marrying anyone I wish to!'

'Oh, no?' Maxim gave a harsh bark of cruel laughter as he strode across the room towards the door. 'I *really* wouldn't bet on it, sweetheart—not if you've got any sense in that beautiful head of yours!'

And then he was gone, only the sound of his sardonic laughter echoing faintly as he ran down the stairs and slammed the front door behind him.

Stephanie sat in her car outside Claire's house in London, trying to pluck up enough courage to knock on the front door.

She didn't want to butt in on Claire's life, but she really didn't have any alternative, did she? She hadn't seen Maxim since he'd slammed his way out of her bedroom five days ago, and with Adam spending the weekend at a friend's house this was the first day she had felt well enough—and the first opportunity she'd had—to get away from the village. The Easter holiday was only a week away, and with the prospect of Claire coming home for the weekend she knew that the gnawing uncertainty about her stepdaughter's relationship with Maxim simply had to be resolved, one way or another.

Come on, don't be such a coward! she berated herself fiercely, finally managing to get out of the car and walk over to the house. Her tentative knock was answered by a tall, thin young man with a violin in one hand and a heavy musical score in the other.

'I think Claire is out in the garden,' he said, pointing vaguely towards a glass-panelled door at the end of the hall.

Nervously opening the door, she walked out on to a small patio, slap bang into the sight of Claire sitting on a garden bench—closely entwined in the arms of a man.

Stephanie's blood ran cold, sickness welling up inside her for a split second before she realised that the man embracing her stepdaughter couldn't possibly be Maxim. The couple were now breaking apart, and she saw that Claire's companion was a tall, handsome young man whom she was quite certain she'd never seen before.

'Hi!' Claire smiled happily as she jumped up from the bench and came over to give Stephanie a kiss on the cheek. 'It's lovely to see you again, but you're looking terribly pale. Are you sure that you've fully recovered from the flu?' she added with concern.

'Yes, I . . .' Stephanie took a deep breath, smiling briefly at the young man who was drawing up a garden chair for her to sit on.

'Oops—sorry!' Claire giggled. 'I haven't introduced you to Paul, have I?'

Suddenly feeling limp and exhausted, Stephanie was profoundly grateful to be able to sit down. Why had she thought, even for one second, that the young man had been Maxim? Oh, lord—she *must* be losing her mind. Because, other than his height, he didn't bear the slightest resemblance to that hard, powerful man, she thought as her gaze swept over the light brown hair and brown eyes of Claire's friend, who was now shaking her hand and introducing himself as Paul Grant.

'Have you been over here long?' she asked, instantly recognising the fact that he was a fellow American.

'No, only for a few months. But I'm planning to stay for a good long time,' he said, smiling broadly at the girl beside him.

Claire beamed back at him, and then grinned at her stepmother. 'Paul and I—well, we're in love! In fact, I suppose we're sort of engaged,' she said, a faint blush staining her cheeks.

'Sort of . . .?' Stephanie echoed blankly, her dazed mind having difficulty in coping with what her stepdaughter was saying. 'Do you mean that you and . . . er . . . Paul are intending to get married?'

'We sure are,' Paul answered. 'Unfortunately, there are just one or two snags that have to be sorted out first. We still haven't thought how to square things up with Maxim. That's the main problem at the moment.'

'*Maxim?*' she exclaimed helplessly. 'What—why should he be involved? I mean, if you two want to get married, I don't see . . .'

Claire laughed. 'Honestly, Stephanie! Don't be so dim. If you're going to marry Maxim . . .'

'Oh, no, I . . .'

'You *must* know that Paul is his son.'

'His stepson, if we're going to be strictly accurate,' Paul said. 'Although I have to admit that Maxim's been a damn good father to me—certainly better than my own would have been, from all accounts.'

'Our two families seem to be crammed full of "steps",' Claire told him with a broad grin. 'What with Maxim being *your* stepfather—and Stephanie *my* stepmother—and the two of *us* being stepchildren . . . well, it's all very complicated, isn't it?'

There was a long silence as Stephanie stared at the young couple, desperately trying to prod her sluggish brain into some sort of working order. But she was barely able to cope with the fact that all her preconceived ideas—all her wildly wrong conclusions and the fearful, barely acknowledged jealousy of her stepdaughter—were now whirling around in her mind like dead leaves in a storm.

'Look,' she said at last, 'can we please take this from the top? I mean, I've never even heard of your existence before today.' She paused, frowning for a moment. 'Oh, yes, I'm sorry—of course I have,' she said, suddenly remembering the telephone call Maxim had taken in his study, the night he'd virtually kidnapped her from the shop and taken her back to his house for dinner. 'You . . . you play the flute, don't you?'

'Yup, I sure do. That's how Claire and I met. And incidentally, I guess I ought to offer you my congratulations. Maxim said he was going to be marrying a beautiful woman, and I can see he wasn't kidding!'

Stephanie's cheeks flushed with annoyance. Why was it that everyone seemed to be so damn certain that she was getting hitched to Maxim? she asked herself angrily. What on earth had he been saying to her stepdaughter and Paul?

Claire stood up. 'I think we all need a strong drink. So, while I see to that, I'll leave Paul to fill you in on his family background, and the story of how we met.' She glanced down at her watch and added, 'No wonder I'm feeling famished, it's way past lunchtime. I'd better make us all some sandwiches, too, while I'm at it.'

As she drove back to the Cotswolds later that after-

noon, Stephanie was still having considerable
difficulty in comprehending the whole complicated story as outlined by Paul Grant, the young man
with whom Claire was so obviously in love.
Luckily, he didn't seem to have any idea that she
had known his stepfather in the past, or that
Adam was Maxim's son. In fact, Paul seemed to
have nothing but a deep fondness and admiration
for the man who had married his widowed
mother, Estelle Grant, when the boy was only
eleven years old.

'My own Dad was a complete workaholic.
Mother and I hardly ever saw him, since he spent
most of his time dashing from one end of the
States to the other. I guess he must have enjoyed
building up his business empire.' Paul had
shrugged. 'But I can't see the point of working that
hard, just to drop dead of a heart attack. One of
the men in Maxim's office block has a sign on his
wall: ''Eat STRESS for breakfast!'' He thinks it's
funny—but I reckon it's just damn stupid. I want
to enjoy my life, not work myself into an early
grave.'

And that, it appeared, was the nub of the
problem. Paul had explained that he felt he owed a
great deal to Maxim. 'In fact, he's been a far better
father to me than my own dad ever was, especially
since my mother was so ill and couldn't really cope
most of the time, but he just can't seem to understand that I'm not interested in Big Business.'

Feeling ashamed of herself, Stephanie hadn't
been able to resist a casual enquiry about his

mother. And then, of course, she wished she hadn't, because Paul seemed to believe she was fully *au fait* with the fact that Estelle Grant had just been diagnosed as having a brain tumour when Paul's father had died.

'Poor Mother, she was really up the creek without a paddle,' Paul had sighed. 'She wasn't just ill—my father's estate was being ripped off by both his own attorney and accountant. There wouldn't have been a damn thing left if Maxim hadn't come galloping to the rescue. He worked for the accountant, and when he discovered what was going on he came to see Mother. He apparently hadn't met her before, and so I guess it was a bit of shock—her being so ill and all.'

'Yes . . . yes, I suppose it must have been,' Stephanie had murmured, feeling totally disorientated. She'd been so wrong about everything else, had she been misjudging Maxim all this time, too?

'Poor Mother, she'd got me and all the business problems—none of which she could cope with, and she was at her wits' end. Of course, it all turned out OK in the end, but she told me once, just a short time before she died, that she never knew where she got the courage to ask Maxim to marry her!' Paul had smiled. 'Still, I guess she must have realised straight away that he's such a soft touch—pure marshmallow underneath that hard, tough exterior. Although I don't have to tell you that, of course,' he had grinned.

Oh, yes, you do! she had wanted to tell him, and had then become so immersed in her own troubled thoughts that she'd almost missed the rest of the story.

It appeared that Paul's father had left a large business empire which, after his marriage to Estelle Grant, had been swiftly and successfully expanded by Maxim into the worldwide conglomerate—Grant-Tyler Corporation. A fact which apparently left Paul completely cold. All he wanted was to pursue a muscial career—an aim which Maxim persistently refused to take seriously. And in an effort to convince his stepson of the virtues of corporate management he had brought Paul over to join him in England.

'And that's where I come into the story,' Claire had said, returning to join them with a tray of beer and sandwiches.

'Paul was hanging around the office one day, and we happened to get talking about music. When I told him that I played the clarinet with a small group of amateur musicians—and it just so happened that the girl who played the flute was leaving to go abroad—well, there was no stopping Paul from joining us! Actually, it's a waste of his time, really, because he's a very talented musician,' Claire had added, leaning over to give him a kiss on the cheek before tucking into her ham sandwich.

It had apparently been Claire's bright idea to be as helpful towards Maxim as possible, in the hope that she would have an opportunity of pleading Paul's case. Which is why she had arranged for Maxim to call in at the Old Barn on his first visit to inspect his new property at Stow-under-Hill—that fateful day when Maxim and Stephanie had met each other again after an absence of so many years.

'I nearly *died* when you asked him how he felt about being a feudal landlord!' Claire grinned. 'I could see the whole of my beautiful scheme whizzing down the plug-hole,' she added, before turning to Paul. 'I honestly don't think I've never seen Stephanie so cold and frosty—and it certainly affected Maxim, because he hardly said a word during the whole of the journey back to London.'

Stephanie grimaced, her face flushing with deep embarrassment as she joined the M4 motorway, and began leaving the suburbs of London behind. There was no doubt that she'd made an *absolute* and *total* fool of herself—adding two and two together and coming up with an answer *so* completely wrong that it made her feel quite sick to even think about what an idiot she'd been.

Even the reason why Claire was leaving her job to work elsewhere was now quite obvious: Maxim feeling that his intention of marrying her stepmother was likely to make her position in his firm a difficult one for the young girl to handle.

But far and away the *most* shaming fact of all was that Stephanie now realised that she had been so totally preoccupied with her own feelings for Maxim, it had never occurred to her that Claire might take a different view.

But, as her stepdaughter had said when kissing her goodbye, 'I do hope you and Maxim will be happy. He's a fantastically clever man—a real financial wizard. And although a lot of women in the office thought he was terrifically attractive, I've never seen it myself.' And then she had frowned. 'Are you sure he isn't too old for you?'

'What on earth are you talking about?' Stephanie had asked, distracted from her intention of making it quite clear that she hadn't yet agreed to marry Maxim.

'Well, he must be at least forty, right? I mean— he's practically got one foot in the grave, hasn't he?'

Stephanie had suddenly found herself convulsed with hysterical laughter, and it wasn't until much later that she realised that she forgotten to tell Claire what she'd been meaning to say.

And that was the sixty-four-thousand-dollar question, wasn't it? What *was* she going to say to Maxim—if and when he ever proposed to her again?

CHAPTER EIGHT

HAVING pulled into a motorway café, where she'd spent a considerable time drinking numerous cups of coffee and thinking hard and long about the problem, Stephanie at last reached Stow-under-Hill as it was beginning to grow dark.

No matter how hard she tried, she couldn't see how it was possible for her to marry Maxim. Paul's disclosures about his mother, and the reasons for Maxim agreeing to marry the poor, unfortunate woman, had been understandable. They had also provided an explanation as to why Maxim had ended their passionate love affair. And, after making such an abysmal fool of herself by coming to one wrong conclusion after another, she had tried to stick to the hard facts of the situation—which brought her little comfort. There was no way she could avoid two obvious conclusions: that Maxim seemed obsessed with gaining some parental control over Adam, and that while he clearly found her physically attractive he had made absolutely no mention of feeling any stronger emotion.

If she didn't love him, maybe there wouldn't be a problem. There was no reason, after all, why two sensible people shouldn't come together to provide a warm home environment for their son. But, unfortunately, she *did* love Maxim, and the torture of having to live with a man who couldn't return her love was more than she could possibly bear. Goodness knows, she was prepared to do just about anything for her son, but agreeing to marry Maxim Tyler was too high a price to pay.

There was no point in sitting around and waiting for Maxim to contact her. Now that she'd made up her mind, it would be far better to get the matter over and done with, she told herself as she drove determinedly on through the village, past her own home, and turned in at the lodge gates of the manor house.

Whether Maxim was at home, she had no idea, but showing none of the trepidation which had affected her when sitting outside Claire's London home Stephanie got out of her car and marched up to the front door.

'Well, well, this is an unexpected pleasure,' Maxim said, surprising her by opening the front door himself.

Stephanie suddenly wished that she hadn't taken the decision to come and see Maxim. It was one thing to make a thoroughly sensible and rational decision not to marry the man—but quite another when the said man was standing so close to her. Even just looking at his tall figure in the slim-fitting dark trousers, his broad shoulders covered by a soft black leather jacket, was enough to make her toes curl. He should carry a government health warning! she thought grimly. Something along the lines of 'Beware—this man is too damn attractive . . .'

would just about fit the bill.

'What's happened to the efficient Mrs Jenkins?' she asked, nervous tension making her voice sound sharper than she intended as he led her across the hall and into the study.

Maxim raised a quizzical dark eyebrow. 'Mrs Jenkins and her husband have worked flat out since I moved into this house. So I've given them the weekend off to go and see their married daughter in Birmingham. All the same,' he paused for a moment, 'if you feel that you require a chaperon, I'm sure I can find someone in the village who . . .'

'Oh, don't be so silly!' she snapped, well aware that despite his bland expression the horrid man's eyes beneath their heavy lids were gleaming with sardonic amusement. 'I didn't come here to talk about Mrs Jenkins,' she said firmly.

'No, of course you didn't,' he agreed smoothly. 'I expect you've come on behalf of the Widows and Orphans Society, hmm?'

'What?' She looked at him in bewilderment.

He shrugged. 'An elderly lady called to see me earlier today, wanting money for an off-beat organisation called the "Distressed Gentlefolk's Association". It just crossed my mind that you might have come to see me on behalf of some charity as well?'

Stephanie gave a shrill, nervous laugh. 'No, of course I haven't.'

'So you're here purely for the sake of my fascinating company? Well, well!'

'No, not exactly,' she murmured evasively,

frowning at the sudden bitter note in his voice, and once again wishing that she hadn't decided to come here this evening. He seemed to be upset about something, and maybe this wasn't a good time to have her say?

'Ah—so there really is a collecting tin hidden beneath that smart dress of yours, hmm?'

'For goodness' sake, Maxim, don't be so ridiculous!' she exclaimed, her cheeks flushing as his gaze travelled slowly down over the curves of her slender body visible beneath the clinging simplicity of her navy-blue dress. 'The reason I've called . . .' She paused and took a deep breath.

'Would you care for a drink?' he asked, just as she was opening her mouth again.

'No, I wouldn't!' she snapped.

'Well, I'm sure you'll forgive me if I help myself?'

Stephanie sighed. She had originally intended to get this meeting over and done with as quickly as possible, but now she had the distinct feeling that it was all somehow going awry—a complete departure from the scenario she'd planned. Waiting impatiently as he took his time over filling his glass, she said, 'Now, if I could get back to what I was about to say . . .'

'Why don't you sit down?' he queried. 'I'm sure you would be far more comfortable than standing there like Joan of Arc at the stake.'

'I'm not . . .' She clicked her teeth with annoyance at being distracted from her purpose. 'Oh, for heaven's sake, will you *please* listen to me?' she demanded as he strolled across the room and sat down in a large, red leather chair.

'I'd really rather not,' Maxim drawled smoothly. 'I know exactly what you're going to say, and I must tell you that I think you're making a great mistake.'

She glared into his handsome face. 'How can you possibly know?'

'Because I know you,' he informed her bluntly. 'You've got yourself all steamed up to come here and tell me that you're not going to marry me.' He shrugged. 'And you're making a big mistake, because—as I told you not so long ago—you're far too lovely to spend the rest of your days playing the role of a virgin widow.'

'Hah! That's all you know!' she ground out, trembling with rage. 'You obviously think you're so damn irresistible—well, let me tell you, that I've decided to get married to someone else—so there!'

'Oh, really?' he drawled, his fingers tightening on his glass as he regarded her with a dangerous gleam in his hard, emerald green eyes. 'And just who, may I ask, is the lucky man?'

'Er—it's Guy,' she lied quickly. She was sorry to have to sacrifice her accountant just to keep her end up with Maxim . . . not that he was going to be her accountant for long, of course. She hadn't heard from Guy after that scene outside her house, and since he had—as Maxim had so unfortunately pointed out—acted like a complete wimp, she had no qualms about taking his name in vain.

'I'm going to marry Guy Fletcher,' she said firmly, staring Maxim straight in the eye. 'We're getting married next week, and we're going to have a really *fabulous* honeymoon, sailing around the Caribbean,' she added, amazed by her own unexpected ability to improvise such an amazing tissue of lies. 'Hmm . . . yes, it's going to be so wonderful,' she cooed, feeling almost intoxicated as she went for the jugular. 'I just can't wait to experience all those lovely hot days—and even *hotter* nights!'

'Don't you play games with me, Stephanie!' he growled, and she realised, when it was far too late, that she'd made a *very* grave mistake.

'OK, Maxim . . . cool down . . . take it easy,' she muttered, edging back towards the door as he erupted from his chair in one fluid, panther-like movement, stalking slowly over the carpet towards her like a dangerous, predatory animal. His face was white beneath the tan, his eyes glittering with ferocious rage.

'You're not going to marry that namby-pamby, wimpish accountant,' he hissed savagely through clenched teeth. 'Not if I've got anything to do with it!'

'OK, OK!' she said hurriedly, continuing to move backwards until she felt the doorknob jar against her spine. Feeling behind her, her fingers frantically sought the edge of the open door as she realised that she must try and escape from this man—who was quite clearly off his head.

'After all the trouble I've had tracking you down, there's *no way* I'm going to let you go now, Stephanie,' he snarled, his hand snaking out and only just missing her as she whirled through the half-open door and ran into the large hall.

Unfortunately her high heels skidded on the slippery surface of the black and white marble floor, and as she staggered, trying to maintain her balance, he moved quickly towards the front door to bar her exit.

'Sorry, *sweetheart*—but you're not going anywhere.' He gave a harsh laugh as he began to walk slowly towards her.

'I'm not going to marry you!' she cried.

'Oh, yes, you are.'

'I . . . I love my son—and I'd do just about anything for him,' her voice quavered as she backed nervously away from his threatening figure, 'but I'm not prepared to sacrifice the rest of my life—just . . . just so you can have a clear conscience!' she added, her voice trembling with fright as she grabbed hold of the large oak newel post and began retreating up the wide staircase.

'I've never heard such—garbage!' He swore violently. 'I didn't even know I had a son—not until a month ago!'

'And that's when you decided you wanted to marry me, right? Just so you could get your hands on Adam!' she panted, quickly backing away up the stairs as he advanced swiftly towards her.

'Oh, really?' he snarled. 'Good lord, Stephanie, how can you be such a remarkably stupid woman? Yes, I was thrilled to learn that I have a son—but it's *you* I want. It's *you* I've been searching for during the last ten years; it's because of *you* that I've bought this damn big house—and come hell or high water, *you are going to marry me*!'

'You're out of your mind! You've really flipped!' she cried, whirling around and dashing swiftly back up the few remaining steps on to the thickly carpeted landing.

Maxim gave a harsh, grating laugh which echoed around the large vaulted landing and deep stairwell. 'Of course I'm out of my mind! What do you expect?' he queried bitterly as he reached the top of the stairs and began moving menacingly towards her. 'I've only ever been in love once in my life. Just once! And when I made the supreme sacrifice— when I realised that I was being monumentally selfish, and that I must turn my back on that love for the very best of reasons . . . what happened?' he demanded savagely. 'Well, I'll tell you, Stephanie. My reward for such virtuous behaviour has been ten long, miserable years containing *nothing*!' he added with a roar of anger. 'Nothing—but dust and ashes!'

Her mind almost paralysed with fright, Stephanie was only dimly beginning to comprehend what he was saying when she realised that his advancing, menacing figure had been herding her, like a stray sheep, towards the only open doorway on the wide landing. Her head swivelling with panic, she looked wildly about her for an avenue of escape. But, even as she was formulating the thought, he moved quickly forward and a split-second later he had seized hold of her, picking her up and throwing her across his broad shoulder like a sack of coal as he strode swiftly into the room.

She had a dazed, blurred impression of cream carpeting and blue walls, and was just opening her mouth to scream for help when she found herself being spun through the air, and the next moment she was lying on a huge four-poster bed, winded and gasping for breath.

'Don't—you—say—one—word! Or I won't be responsible for my actions,' he snarled through clenched teeth, and Stephanie quailed at the terrifying menace projected by the rigid, tense figure staring so threateningly down at her.

There was a long, emotionally charged silence in the room as they stared at one another, before Maxim, barely controlling his rage and anger, began stripping off his leather jacket.

'I've *never* lost my temper like that before—certainly not as far as I can remember!' he breathed savagely, tossing the jacket on to a nearby armchair. 'You certainly have a lot to answer for, Stephanie,' he added, unknotting his tie with swift, taut movements. 'What in the hell do you think you were doing—deliberately winding me up with all that stupid nonsense about marrying your wimpish, lily-livered accountant?'

She couldn't speak. It seemed as if her vocal cords were paralysed as she stared, mesmerised, at the harsh expression on his face, almost drowning in the glittering cold fire of his emerald green eyes.

'Well?' he demanded roughly.

'I guess I wanted to . . . to hurt you,' she whispered, not able to stop herself from shaking like a leaf, and with her heart pounding so loudly that she felt certain he must be able to hear it.

'Well, sweetheart, you sure succeeded!' He gave a grim laugh.

'I'm sorry . . .' she breathed, her eyes widening with alarm as she saw he was beginning to unbutton his shirt, a shiver running through the length of her body at the sight of the dark hairs on his deeply tanned chest. But, as she tried to scramble off the bed, her reactions proved to be far slower than his. With what seemed to be the speed of light he had grabbed hold of her, and a moment later he was pinning her to the soft mattress with his hard, firm body.

She tried to struggle, to push him away, but all to no avail. He was too powerful, far too determined as he captured her lips beneath the burning pressure of his mouth. She could hardly breathe as his tongue plundered the inner softness of her mouth in a devastating invasion of her shattered senses. There was no resistance she could make to his superior strength and, quite suddenly, she knew that she didn't want to.

What was the point of continuing to fight against the deep love she had for this man? Why deny her desperate hunger and longing to feel his hard figure pressed so closely to hers? And then she realised that Maxim must have sensed her surrender, felt her rigid body softening and melting beneath him, because the bruising force of his mouth began to ease, his lips gently moving over hers before he slowly and reluctantly raised his head.

'I'm sorry—I didn't mean to frighten you just now,' he muttered huskily, staring down at her pale cheeks. Time seemed to hang suspended as she saw the topaz lights in his pupils slowly enlarge, glowing feverishly as his eyes moved over her trembling lips and the cloud of ash-blonde hair shining like pale moonlight as it flowed over the soft blue bedcover.

'I chose the colour of this bedroom to match your lovely blue eyes,' he murmured, his own eyes blazing fiercely in the dim light as he cupped her face with hands that shook and trembled with barely controlled tension. 'Oh, how I love you, Stephanie. These past ten years have been such torture!' he rasped hoarsely, a deep groan torn from his throat as he buried his face in the soft fragrance of her hair.

It was some time before he brought himself under control, rolling off her soft body to lie on his back beside her, and staring blindly up at the ruched silk lining the top of the four-poster bed.

'I've never forced a woman in my life—and I don't aim to start now,' he muttered thickly, brushing a trembling hand across his eyes. 'So, after you've had a good laugh at what a damned fool I've made of myself—why don't you just get the hell out of here, huh?'

'Oh, no—if there's a prize idiot around here, I'm afraid it's me,' Stephanie whispered huskily, turning on to her side and raising a tentative hand to brush a lock of dark hair from his brow. 'I . . . I've never been able to stop loving you, however hard I've tried. And I . . . well, I guess I just haven't been seeing straight—looking down the wrong end of the telescope—ever since you came back into my life. Oh, Maxim!' she wailed, her eyes filling with tears and yet unable to tear her gaze away from his wide, sensual mouth, the warmth and tenderness of the expression now spreading over his face. 'You've *no* idea of just how foolish I've been. I . . .'

'Don't cry, my love,' he murmured softly, gathering her into his arms. 'I promise you that I'll never give you any cause to weep again.'

His lips found hers in a kiss of such gentle, piercing sweetness that she thought she would almost die of happiness. And when at last Maxim lifted his mouth from hers, she couldn't speak, her arms closing about him, her fingers curling into his thick black hair as she drew him urgently back down towards her. He drew a deep, unsteady breath, his hands slowly moving over the body trembling beneath him, the heat of his fingers as they lingered on the full sweetness of her breasts almost scorching through the thin material of her dress.

He was handling her, she thought dizzily, as if she were a piece of very rare, precious glass, but she wanted more. There was nothing in the world she wanted more than his possession. Burning with desire, her need of him so intense that it was like a deep physical pain, she arched against him in an age-old, instinctive gesture of invitation, her body quivering in response as she felt the full force of his desire.

'Stephanie . . .' he groaned, desperately trying to maintain control of his emotions. But the floodtide of her desire was relentless, urgently demanding a release from the hot, aching need that surged through her veins.

A deep shudder vibrated through his large frame at the increasingly erotic, sensual motion of her body as it moved so enticingly beneath him. The provocation proving too strong for him to combat as he gave a low growl and, firmly in the grip of a primitive force that was quite beyond either of them to control, he quite literally tore the clothes from first her body and then his. The raw, savage emotion which had been repressed for so long exploded passionately between them, and she was too lost in physical sensation to hear the cry that rippled from her own throat as their bodies merged in the wild, untamed hunger of their overpowering need for each other; only conscious of the raw power of his thrusting possession, which shattered her senses as he swept her up over the precipice into the free-fall of passionate ecstasy and true fulfilment.

Later, as they lay warmly and drowsily entwined together, Maxim raised his head from the deep valley of her breasts, raising his hand to turn her face gently towards him. 'I'm sorry if I was too rough, sweetheart,' he murmured. 'I just couldn't seem to control myself, I . . .' He shook his head.

'Hell—you're some woman!'

'You're pretty amazing yourself, Mr Tyler!' Stephanie gave him a sleepy smile, still feeling dazed by the passion which had leaped so fiercely between them, and astonished by the force of her own response to his frenzied lovemaking. Even now, as he bent his dark head to trace lazy patterns with his lips upon her full breasts, she could feel faint tremors of desire beginning to flow through her veins once again.

Oh, lord—I wonder if I'm turning into one of those crazy nyphomaniacs? she thought, and it wasn't until she felt him shaking with laughter that she realised she had spoken aloud.

'I won't complain if you do,' he told her with a loving grin. 'Incidentally, I hope that you're going to make an honest man of me—at long last?'

She realised from the slight tensing of his body that he still wasn't entirely sure of her answer. 'Oh, Maxim—yes, of course I'm going to marry you!' she cried, anxious to wipe the faint shadow from his face as she gave him a fervent kiss. 'It's just . . . well, there have been so many misunderstandings between us that I guess I couldn't see the wood for the trees.'

'You're not the only one,' he said soberly. 'I must have made every mistake in the book—ever since I attended a dull charity reception in New York, and quite suddenly and dramatically fell in love with the most beautiful young girl I had ever seen. I felt as though I'd been given the whole world, and for a few brief days I was almost literally walking on air—

happier than I guess any mortal man has a right to be. And who knows?' He gave an unhappy shrug. 'Maybe all those ancient Greek tragedies aren't so far from the truth, hmm? I've often wondered if maybe we were *too* happy—too much in love? Well, if so, I guess we've sure paid for it since.' He sighed heavily, brushing a hand roughly through his dark hair.

'Oh, darling,' she murmured, putting her slim arms about him for a moment. 'Why didn't you tell me the truth about your wife, right at the beginning?'

Maxim gave an unhappy shrug. 'I . . . I don't really know how to describe what happened to me. One minute I was going through the usual polite cocktail party conversation with people who were equally as bored as I was—and then I looked across the room at you, and . . . well, I guess the best way to describe it, sweetheart, is to say that it seemed as if "time" didn't exist any more; as if all the clocks in the world had immediately stopped ticking . . .' He sighed heavily.

'If I'm honest, I guess the truth is that I was so desperately in love—snatching greedily at my first real chance of joy and happiness, that I was simply oblivious of all my normal family duties and responsibilities. For most of those treasured, precious five days we had together, I was totally out of touch with reality—and then I eventually came back down to earth, and began to realise the terrible harm and damage I was likely to cause by my irresponsible behaviour. I knew it wouldn't be possible to keep the fact that I was married a secret for very long. And once you found out the truth—as you were bound to eventually—then what?' He gave her an unhappy, crooked smile. 'Even if you hadn't ended our relationship immediately, you were so young and innocent, with all your life in front of you—how could I ask you to put up with what would have been at best a part-time love affair as my mistress?

'Poor Estelle . . . I should never have married her, of course.' He sighed and pushed a hand roughly through his black hair. 'But she was in such desperate trouble over her late husband's estate; she knew she didn't have long to live, and was almost out of her mind with worry about what would happen to her young son. I was so damn sorry for the poor woman . . .' Maxim sighed heavily again, falling silent for a moment. 'And then, two years later, I met you. But Estelle was so dreadfully ill, and had been through so many operations—there was no way I could possibly walk out on her and my young stepson, to have made her life any more hellish than it was already. And I told myself that if I *really* loved you, I'd let you go. That I wouldn't ruin your life with an affair that could never blossom into marriage.'

'Oh, Maxim!' There was anguish in Stephanie's voice. 'You should have known that I'd have waited for you forever—until the end of time, if need be!'

Maxim shook his head and said softly, 'No, sweetheart. I couldn't have asked that of you. It would have been wicked to try and persuade you to live such a sterile existence.' He sighed and lay back on the pillows. 'When I left you, I truly thought I was making the only right and proper decision—although, heaven knows, I felt as though I was bleeding to death the night I walked out of your apartment.'

'I was absolutely devastated,' she whispered, burying her face in his shoulder. 'And then to find that I was expecting your baby . . .' She shuddered at the memory of that unhappy time.

He groaned huskily, his arms tightening protectively about her slim body. 'If only I'd known! I'll never be able to forgive myself for abandoning you in that condition,' he said thickly. 'But I had absolutely no idea—believe me, darling, it simply *never* crossed my mind that I could have given you a baby . . .' He sighed and shook his head at his own stupidity. 'After Estelle died—and I was free to marry again—I moved heaven and earth to try and find you; but there was someone else living in your apartment, and none of your neighbours had any idea of where you'd gone. Goodness knows how many thousands of dollars I must have spent on trying to trace you, but it seemed as though you'd vanished off the face of the globe. And I *still* don't know what really happened to you before you landed up here in this village.'

'I met James a few weeks after you left, and . . .' She hesitated, quickly deciding not to tell him about the unhappy circumstances in which she'd first met the Englishman. Maxim hadn't known she was

pregnant, and there was no sense in giving him any
reason to be even more wretched about abandoning
her than he was already. So she merely confined
herself to a brief outline of her decision to move to
England, and her subsequent marriage to James
Hammond. 'It was such a shock when you suddenly turned up with Claire—such an extraordinary
coincidence!' she exclaimed.

'Coincidence?' He gave a deep rumble of laughter. 'It was hardly that! I'd managed to track you
down well over two years ago. It was trying to find
a way of grabbing hold of you—to manoeuvre you
into marrying me—that was the real problem.'

'What!' She struggled to sit up, her eyes wide
with astonishment. 'Do you mean to tell me . . .?'

'Oh, sure—it was a set-up, sweetheart!' He
grinned, laughing as she angrily beat her fists on his
chest. 'Now, that's enough,' he said, capturing her
wrists and drawing her once more into his arms for
a long, passionate kiss. 'I really went to some
lengths for your sake, you know,' he added a few
moments later. 'Buying that large corporation in
London wasn't exactly accomplished in a day—and
this estate didn't come cheap, either!'

'But why?' she demanded breathlessly. 'Why on
earth did you go to such lengths? Surely you could
have just flown over to see me—knocked on the
door and said "hello", or something like that?'

'Oh, sure,' he grimaced. 'And you'd have
welcomed me with open arms, huh?'

'Well . . .'

'Yes, that's exactly what I thought. And look at it

from my side of the fence. You'd been totally lost to me until one day, when I was in the office of a clothing firm I'd just taken over, I saw your picture in a trade magazine which was lying open on the desk. I nearly fainted! When I got my head back together again, I employed investigators on this side of the Atlantic to find out all they could—which wasn't a great deal. I knew you'd married that guy, James, that you had two stepchildren and a son by your husband, and that you were now a widow running a shop and a handknitting business here in the Cotswolds. So I thought—right, I'll buy up the firm that's selling her clothes in the States . . .'

'Harold!' she exclaimed, suddenly remembering the conversation with her father's old friend so many weeks ago.

'And then I had a better idea. I didn't know much about your life-style, but I reckoned it would be difficult to uproot you from this country—especially as your son was apparently at boarding-school. So I decided to move my centre of operations to London.'

'It all seems a bit . . . well, a bit extreme,' she murmured, shaking her head in bewilderment.

He drew her closer to his warm body. 'Don't you understand?' he murmured thickly, burying his face in the cloudy tangle of her blonde hair. 'I *knew* that you only fall in love, as I did, once in a lifetime. And that if I made one false move, I might lose you again. So there was no expense I wouldn't have gone to, not if it meant our being together again. I was so desperate to get hold of you that I didn't

even care that you'd been married to another man
and had a child by him.'

'But I didn't . . .'

'Yes, I know that now, but at the time I naturally
assumed that Adam was James Hammond's son.'

'No, that's not what I meant.' Her cheeks
flushed. 'I . . . I never . . . James and I didn't . . .'
She took a deep breath. 'You're the only man
who's ever made love to me.'

'Oh, *Stephanie*!' he groaned. 'I wasn't telling the
truth just now. I've been so tortured—almost
driven crazy with jealousy. But I knew I had no
right . . .' His mouth claimed hers in a deeply
possessive, passionate kiss that seemed to last forever. When at last he let her go, she lay flushed and
breathless in his arms.

'Darling one, please understand that I didn't
know much about your private life when I bought
the firm in London—but there was one outstanding
coincidence in this whole affair, of course. When I
went through the staff list and saw Claire's name, I
knew the gods were on my side! I can tell you, that
girl was promoted to my personal office so quickly
that I don't think she knew what had hit her!' He
laughed. 'And it was through her that I heard this
estate was for sale. Everything was going along
nicely when I suddenly had my come-uppance.' He
gave a shaky grin. 'I was practically in terminal
shock when I realised Adam had to be my son! But
his existence gave me the perfect opportunity to put
pressure on you.'

'Yes, you certainly did pile on the pressure!' she

retorted grimly. 'I've never been so mentally exhausted and worn out in my whole life.'

'I know, darling, and I'm truly sorry—but I couldn't see how I had any alternative. Especially with that damn accountant hanging around,' Maxim added darkly. 'My investigators had told me that he seemed to be becoming a fixture in your life, so I had to get rid of him—*fast*!'

Stephanie gave an exasperated sigh. 'Oh, you certainly did that, all right! I should think my name's mud in Broadway.'

'Sorry, sweetheart.' He grinned.

'You rotten liar! You're not a bit sorry,' she grumbled. 'But what about my good name?'

'Your "good name" is now going to be Mrs Tyler, and as my dearly beloved wife you can rest assured that I'm not likely to allow *any* gossip to touch you —or my son,' he said firmly. 'I'm so thrilled about Adam.' His voice softened as he brushed a stray curl from her brow. 'I can see I'm going to have a hard time not to spoil him stupid! I'm very fond of Paul, of course,' he added quickly. 'I more or less brought him up, and we're very close. But to have conceived a son of my own . . .' He sighed happily. 'Well, I guess that sort of makes him a very special person as far as I'm concerned.'

'Since you've mentioned Paul . . .' She hesitated. 'I haven't had a chance to tell you, but I met him today. At Claire's house.'

'Yes, I believe the two of them are quite good pals —which is going to make a really good family atmosphere for us all, right?'

Stephanie grinned. 'You're more "right" than you realise! Because, my darling Machiavellian husband-to-be, while you've been so busy scheming on *your* own account, there have been some other—er—developments. I don't know how you're going to feel about it, but Claire and Paul are intending to get married as well!'

Maxim threw back his head and roared with laughter. 'Oh, that's just great! Tell me all about it.'

And when she had finished explaining how the two young people had come together, she added, 'You've got to face it, Maxim. Paul really isn't interested in high finance, and I think that it's probably cruel to keep trying to force his nose to the business grindstone.'

'Don't worry, I've already come to the same conclusion,' Maxim assured her. 'Besides,' he grinned, 'I've got another son to take over from me now, haven't I? Although I must confess that I've already found myself wondering just what Adam, with that brain of his, would do to my business—and I'm profoundly grateful that it will be some years before I find out!' he laughed.

'But how are we going to tell Adam that you're his father?' she asked, a worried note in her voice.

He smiled gently down at her. 'I don't want to make the mistake of rushing into giving him the news too soon—and I also realise that we mustn't leave it too late. So, if we take care to explain that he was conceived by two people who loved each other very much, but who were temporarily unable to get married, I'm hopeful that it won't be too much of a shock. But let's cross that bridge when we get to it, hmm?' he murmured, raising a hand to tenderly brush a stray lock of hair from her face.

'Oh, lord!' she gasped, catching a glimpse of the time on his wristwatch. 'Adam has being staying with a friend, and I'd arranged to pick him up over half an hour ago. What on earth am I going to do?'

'Don't worry. We'll ring them up and say you've been delayed, and then we'll both go and fetch him.'

Stephanie gave a wry laugh. 'Oh, I'm not worried about being late—it's what I'm going to wear that's the problem!' She put out a hand and lifted up the tattered fragments of her dress.

'Did I really do that?' He gave her a shame-faced grin.

'Mmm, you sure did!' Her cheeks flushed at the memory of their overwhelmingly passionate encounter. 'If that's the way you're going to make love to me in the future—well, it's just as well that you're a wealthy man. My clothes are going to cost you a fortune!'

'It will be worth every cent,' he assured her, lying back on the pillows and sighing with pleasure. 'I'm not just a wealthy man. Far more important, I'm a supremely *happy* man. I'm going to be married as soon as possible to the most wonderful woman in the world. So, I ask you, what more has life to offer me?'

Stephanie looked at him with loving exaspera-tion. 'If I can't find something to wear in the next five minutes—life, in the shape of myself, is going to offer you a thump on the nose!'

'Don't worry,' he murmured, rolling over to trap her soft body beneath him, his mouth possessing her lips in a long tender kiss. 'Finding something to cover your delicious shape is peanuts compared to all I've gone through to make you my own—at last! So relax. When I've finished kissing you, I'll definitely guarantee to come up with an answer.'

And, of course, he did.

RW

Have You Ever Wondered If You Could Write A Harlequin Novel?

Here's great news—Harlequin is offering a series of cassette tapes to help you do just that. Written by Harlequin editors, these tapes give practical advice on how to make your characters—and your story—come alive. There's a tape for each contemporary romance series Harlequin publishes.

Mail order only

All sales final
